The PARIS YEARS of ROSIE KAMIN

The Paris Years of Rosie Kamin

RICHARD TELEKY

STEERFORTH PRESS
SOUTH ROYALTON, VERMONT

For information about permission to reproduce selections
from this book, write to: Steerforth Press L.C.,
P.O. Box 70, South Royalton, Vermont 05068.

Library of Congress Cataloging-in-Publication Data

Teleky, Richard, 1946-
The Paris years of Rosie Kamin / Richard Teleky.
p. cm.
ISBN 1-883642-96-5 (alk. paper)
I. Title
PR9199.3.T417P37   1998
813'.54—dc21   97-47402
                         CIP

The text of this book was composed by Steerforth Press
using a digital version of Sabon.

This novel is a work of fiction. Names, characters, places, and
incidents are either the products of the author's imagination
or are used fictitiously. Any resemblance to actual persons,
living or dead, events, or locales is entirely coincidental.

Special thanks to Dr. Sharon Salloum, who kindly read this
novel in manuscript with an attentive medical eye.
— R. T.

Manufactured in the United States of America

FIRST EDITION

For Anita

1

*R*OSIE HAD LIVED IN PARIS for twenty years, but she still debated which Métro station to use. Though Riquet was her official stop, as she told first-time visitors, she often got off at Crimée or Stalingrad to vary the route. Crimée had the bridge, the *pont levant,* and was closer to her apartment; Stalingrad had the eighteenth-century rotunda. Nine years before, after she moved into the nineteenth arrondissement, Rosie had shoved a handful of postcards of Place Stalingrad in the bottom of a bureau drawer. She was going to send them to her people back home — her father, Deb, Uncle Aladar — but on settling down to address them she had wondered if anyone would care. Crimée was the better station. Why didn't they sell a postcard of its lovely old bridge?

With no reason to hurry, Rosie left the Métro at Riquet. The Sunday afternoon crowd had thinned; everyone with a place to go was already there. Two North African women in faded robes stood talking at the bottom of the desolate white-tile stairwell, and as Rosie passed them the heel-strap of her right shoe gave out. She looked down at her feet. Eight hundred francs gone. She always wore these shoes without stockings, like sandals.

Rosie twisted her right foot in the shoe to keep it on — even with her shoes secure on her feet she dreaded climbing the steep Métro stairway or crossing Paris's wide boulevards. Then she looked at her watch. The charcuterie on her corner would still be open. A few slices of smoked ham, maybe some leeks vinaigrette. She wasn't particularly hungry, but before she left the hospital Serge had reminded her to eat something.

If he were home, they might even have gone to one of the small shops in the Marais for the spicy sausages he loved. And some pastries for her. Rosie didn't understand why people made such a fuss over those light French concoctions, tasting of air; she liked the rich, heavy kind filled with apricot purée or poppy seeds. Yet when Serge teased that her preference showed she was a good Jew after all, she felt annoyed. The best thing about Judaism, Rosie thought, was the food. But you couldn't base a life on it, although her family had tried.

Half limping — the shoe had a will of its own — Rosie turned onto rue de Flandre, passing the tobacco shop, the boulangerie, the computer store that used to be a millinery shop, the North African café where couples sat engrossed in each other. Even with someone at your side, Sunday in Paris was the loneliest day of the week. Rosie recalled a tin of Danish biscuits one of her students had given her last month; maybe she'd just have some of those, with coffee. The café was unadorned, awaiting renovation. She and Serge had gone there during Ramadan and watched men play bingo for what seemed fairly sizeable stakes.

The nineteenth was changing. Algerians and Africans, Vietnamese and Cambodians mingled with the French. There was a new Hebrew school that belonged to a community of North African Jews, and even a falafel shop, though no kosher butcher. Not that Rosie cared. Serge had heard of a small, old Jewish cemetery hidden in the court-yard of an apartment building, but they'd never managed to find it. The canal quarter faced rising rents and property values — an invasion of the middle class. It hadn't changed as much as the streets around Buttes Chaumont, the park Napoleon had built for a mistress, but it wasn't the same.

As usual Rosie ignored the block-long apartment building to her left, a cement and white-tile monstrosity looming over the street like a sinking ocean liner. Instead she looked at the shop windows on her side of the street. She knew their contents as well as those of her kitchen shelves. Despite Serge's promptings, she refused to use the new supermarket in the base of the monster building. Surrounded by a sea of renovations, she preferred the surviving old shops. She had to make a gesture. Maybe she would stop at the charcuterie for a stuffed tomato. Without Serge, there was no reason to hurry. Later she would try out the new shampoo from the clinic. Rosie had unusually fine black hair, and small patches of it on the left side of her head had recently begun to fall out. "What if I go completely bald?" she'd cried to Serge, who assured her that wouldn't happen. But Rosie barely heard him. The doctor said it was probably caused by *le stress*.

She dug into her black string bag, found her change purse between the newspapers and a pad of writing paper, and entered the charcuterie. At least she would eat well before trying the shampoo. She'd opened it yesterday at the hospital and the smell was awful. Serge had apologized for not being able to help: "I'd dry your hair so gently, none of it would fall out." The shampoo's tar base caused the odor, unpleasant, sickening. Would he smell it on her hair tomorrow?

In the charcuterie she stood before white enamel trays of hors d'oeuvres, remembering how she'd enjoyed making her

3

choices, taking them home and carefully placing them on the Moroccan plates. Someone from school had told her that the blue glaze Moroccan potters use contained too much lead and could poison you, but Rosie didn't have the heart to throw the plates out. People said all kinds of things.

The couple ahead of her, in their mid-thirties, held hands while debating the virtues of one cheese over another, their voices caressing the names. Rosie turned away; they could own the world without her. Serge had suggested she go to a movie. One of the rep houses was playing *The Lady from Shanghai* — "Tell me about it," he'd said — but Rosie was certain he knew that she wouldn't go. Maybe she'd write to Deb. Her sister had recently written to say that she'd won a trip to Paris for two.

"Madame?" a voice repeated from behind the counter.

Rosie ordered, wishing she could ask someone to help. The proprietor was French, but even though she'd been shopping here for nine years she couldn't say, "If you came to the hospital with me and asked the doctor what was wrong . . . you know how they look at you when you're not French . . . then I can't think of anything to say." Of course she couldn't say that.

Maybe she would consider the movie after all, Rosie thought, pocketing her change. But she wasn't particularly interested in old American movies, even though the French made a fetish of them. When everyone in Paris began watching *Dallas*, she'd felt it as a personal affront. "I've never seen it," she'd say firmly, if asked. She hadn't stayed in France for twenty years only to end up watching *Dallas*.

Back on the street she heard a wail of Eastern music from the café, where someone must have turned up the stereo. A Mercedes was now parked by the curb, and a boy of about twelve — Vietnamese? Cambodian? — stood kicking a rear tire, while the café customers pretended to ignore him.

Rosie walked more quickly as she approached her street, Duverger. Its name — of the orchard — had once amused her, for in the early nineteenth century this neighborhood had been a vast garbage dump that people said infected all Paris with its stench. Now the irony of the name had worn off. It might even be heartening to live on a street named after a sewer. The other tenants in her building were North Africans, a Turkish family, and a married Italian couple whose dog regularly shat on the staircase, but apart from Serge only a few French people. At least one apartment was reserved by the town hall for former prisoners. Rosie hated coming home alone late at night, when North African men from the street lingered there talking, and she had to avoid their glances with apparent calm. But winter, when Duverger was deserted, held other problems. Squatters often occupied any vacant apartment on the block, which meant a rash of burglaries.

Tonight several cars had parked illegally, crowding the narrow street, and in one of them a young couple sat, the radio blaring. Exhausted by the afternoon, Rosie gave her right shoe one final twist — it might be easier to carry it, but people spat on the streets and you never knew what to expect on the staircase. It was hot for an early June night.

She entered her building, switched on the stairwell light and took a deep breath. Her apartment was at the top, on the fifth floor. If she hurried the light wouldn't go out before she got there. Watching her feet, Rosie saw no evidence of the Ferronis' dog. She had been raised in a family that wouldn't allow even the thought of a pet, and still believed all animals were unclean.

She paused for an instant and heard someone on the staircase above her. The sound of breathing increased with each step she took, and she was about to call out just as the light flickered. She had almost recognized the man, seated on the stairs with his head bowed. She couldn't see his face, but she knew the small head and the thick dark brown hair. She held her bags close to her side as the light flickered a second time. He looked up and said, "Rosie?"

"Benyoub?"

How many years since they'd spoken? Five, six?

She sighed with relief and fumbled for her keys while he stood up, blocking the way. Two steps higher, he was tall for a moment. As usual he wore a crisp white shirt. "How did you find my address?" she asked.

"Does it matter?"

"I'm just curious." She pushed past him and turned the key in the lock.

"All right, then. In a dream."

She laughed in spite of herself, and he laughed too. She had a small round chin and full lips that gave her face a natural pout even when she felt happy.

The door opened into a stifling room where afternoon sun had beat on the roof, baking the apartment.

"It was supposed to rain," Rosie said, "or I wouldn't have shut the windows."

Cluttered with heavy old furniture, and books piled several feet high along the baseboards, the room apparently surprised Benyoub, who remained in the doorway.

"You were shopping?" he asked, glancing at her bag. "I've been waiting for an hour."

"Well, I wasn't expecting you. If you're coming in, close the door. I have to put these things in the kitchen — sit down anywhere."

Benyoub followed her across the room. "Can I help?"

"I just have to put this in the refrigerator." She wouldn't offer him a drink, although she wanted one herself.

He stood at the kitchen door, watching her. "Are we going to have a glass of wine?" he suggested. "We could go out if you'd like."

She no longer had time for men who appeared and disappeared without explanation. They belonged to the years when it seemed that everyone she knew was a graduate student in sociology. "Which Greek tragedy have you been reliving?" she asked.

"Come give me a friendly kiss."

Arrogance and charm still intact.

"We could go out, you know."

"This isn't a date, Ben. I didn't invite you here."

He actually managed to look wounded — maybe he even believed it.

During their five years together sleep had been Rosie's best companion. Before him she'd had to contend with so many selfish men it was easier to close up and sleep, dependent on Ben. Unfair all around, but she'd seen no other way. How many times had she told friends, "He's been back in Algeria for a couple of weeks, working out some problems"? And then, inevitably, "I wrote quite a harsh letter to Algeria."

He had a secretive nature and a need for solitude that excluded her. "We don't live like a couple," she'd say. "There's something wrong with you," he'd reply. "You always have me on your mind." "What's wrong with that?" she'd answer.

She had explained him often enough to friends: It wasn't his fault that being on a student visa meant he couldn't get a French work permit or a decent job; he didn't want to be a student forever. Maybe it didn't make sense to try to live in Paris, but what alternative did he have? (Friends couldn't answer.) He was a gentle person who had proved his affection for her; he just hated domestic life. It wasn't his fault that she saw him too little, that she waited so pitifully for him to come back, to be ready for her. His every criticism pained her, yet when she finally decided to leave him they reached a truce that lasted several months. He gave what he could, preparing delightful spiced meals of cous-cous that he quietly put aside for when she came home. No longer impatient, cold, silent, he would tease her the way he used to in their early days together. (Rosie liked to be teased.) "Hey, you, American Leftie, why do you romanti-cize the Algerian government? The people hate it." Then Rosie would reply that she'd been written out of the Amer-ican way of things. Together they'd read the Rosenbergs' let-ters from prison.

"I needed to see you," he began, following her into the living room. She settled in a corner of the sofa and he sat beside her familiarly.

She had no patience left. "So you want something, is that it?"

"It's not wrong to want things."

"From me it is."

He stared at her as if she'd lost control, with a look of fatalism she remembered too well. How many others had heard the story he was preparing to tell?

"Why are you making that face?" he asked.

Rosie knew she ought to be careful. Benyoub at thirty-five — five years younger than Rosie — still had the boyish quality she once said he used to win people over. Enigmatic Ben, the troubled boy. She'd seen him on the street a few times since moving into Serge's apartment, but always man-aged to avoid a meeting. The last time they spoke face-to-face — on a miserable January day in 1985 — she'd even loaned him three thousand francs. In his predictably charm-ing manner he promised to return most of it by the end of April. When he hadn't contacted her by June, she sent sev-eral notes, and he finally telephoned, committing himself to Bastille Day. In the end, he returned the loan a year later. It seemed almost normal. After leaving him she felt freer, but selfish, not having to consider his needs.

"Do you live here alone?" he asked, looking about openly.

"No."

"It doesn't seem like your place."

"What do you mean?"

"All this old furniture."

When Serge bought the apartment it was already cluttered with ponderous furniture from the thirties, and he managed to add even more, joking that there wasn't a single good piece in sight. Rosie had persuaded him to drag an ugly buffet into the bedroom, to use for storage, and then gave up. Once or twice a year she would decide to rid the apartment of all its serviceable, old rust-colored upholstery, which had faded to mud brown, but somehow the moment of transformation never arrived. She confined her decorating attempts to linens, plants, colorful pillows, and the kitchen. While Rosie sometimes called the apartment "my flea market," she would never use the term to Benyoub.

"You're a decorator now? I thought you studied sociology."

"Rosie, aren't you even going to give me a friendly kiss?"

"That table belonged to Serge's great-grandmother."

"Serge?"

"The man I live with."

"A Russian?"

"No. His name's Serge, not Sergei. It's French." Poor Serge. Foreigners often assumed he was Russian, which amused him since he was a Communist.

"Where is he?"

"In the hospital."

Benyoub leaned forward, placing his elbows on his knees and clasping his hands. Serge sat that way too, Rosie thought. She couldn't remember ever seeing a woman sit like that.

9

"Can I help you?" he asked. "Is there anything I can do?"

She knew he meant it. "Nothing."

"Is it serious?"

"I don't think so. Something about his liver." Rosie ran her fingers through the hair over her left ear. Definitely thinner than last week.

"Then it could be serious."

"Don't say that. He's going to be all right." The vehemence of her voice startled her.

"I only meant . . ."

"I don't like it when people say things like that. He's going to be fine. They said he could come home in a week."

"Which hospital?"

"Tenon. In the twentieth."

"I don't know it," he said.

"I didn't either. Until he went there."

"You're sure there's nothing I can do?"

"Why do you keep asking?"

"I'm not exactly a refugee. I know things. People." His eyes could still draw her in — almost. He offered himself through them.

"I never said you didn't."

He stared at his hands. When they first met, in a café, she told him she'd written a university paper on Fanon's *The Wretched of the Earth*. "All the girls tell me that," he'd said, dismissively, but from the tone of his voice she'd known they would sleep together that night.

"What are you smiling at?"

"I was thinking of Frantz Fanon. Does anyone read him today?"

"How would I know?"

"When you go home, I mean back to Algeria, do people still talk about him?"

"What makes you think I go back to Algeria?"

"You used to."

"I didn't come here to talk about Fanon. This is difficult for me."

She waited. When they'd lived together she'd had the small apartment on rue de Charenton, and if their schedules didn't coincide, or if one was sleeping, the other felt paralyzed. Benyoub worked as a night clerk in a dirty hotel, from eight in the evening to six in the morning, and Rosie would visit him there every night around eleven, bringing sandwiches for them to share. "Are you working now?"

He shook his head. "I have serious problems."

"And?"

"I don't want to go into them. There's no point in boring you."

"Where are you living?"

He shrugged.

"Ben? You must have friends."

"Why do people always ask if I have friends here? You know friends don't last long in Paris."

On this they agreed. But Rosie also remembered that the people around Benyoub were often vague, disconnected, troubled. Like Ben himself. Weekends, she'd been afraid to disturb him during the day, so she'd stay out of the apartment while he slept, coming home only to cook supper, which they ate sitting cross-legged on the bed. Usually he was still wearing the striped pajamas she'd given him, and they fed each other apricots, told stories, made love. Usually he stayed in.

"Sometimes," she said, leaning back, "when I think of the people I've fallen out with, or stopped seeing, it seems that making real friends is a mystery. It's all beyond your control."

"Don't bring God into this."

"We have a Muslim grocer who claims that whenever he wants something he prays to Allah, and Allah always comes through. For years I've wanted to ask him if Allah listens to Jews, too. Or women."

"Why don't you?"

Rosie laughed. "I've been collecting grievances for a while."

Benyoub stood and crossed the room to a window that overlooked the street. Rosie wondered what he was thinking. She used to accuse him of identifying with women's problems of a psychological rather than practical nature.

"Can you help me with some money?" he asked. "I need at least twenty thousand francs."

"That's a lot."

"I know. But you're surrounded by nice things, you've got a real home. Maybe your friend Serge would help."

"Why would Serge help?"

"Does he know about me?"

"Of course. We weren't children when we met. But that's beside the point."

"Does he know about Hamed, too?"

"Why bring him up?"

"I just wondered."

"Well I don't like it. What right do you have coming here and . . ."

"I don't have any rights. That's the trouble. I wouldn't bother you if I had a choice."

"Okay. I'm sorry."

"Are you going to help me?"

He didn't look at her, and Rosie was grateful.

2

*W*HENEVER ROSIE TRIED to remember her mother, she hit a wall. Elza had done her best to conceal herself from her daughters and her husband. "My past's past," she used to say. But Rosie knew a few things.

Born in Budapest, Elza had been sent to Auschwitz with her father, where he'd been killed. Her mother, Roza, had died shortly before Hungary began interning its Jews, but when Rosie — who had been named after her grandmother — asked of what, Elza would never explain: "She died, that's all." This was said softly, as a matter of fact. And Elza also refused to discuss her life in Auschwitz, or the refugee camp afterward, or how her brother Aladar in Pittsburgh had finally sponsored her to come to America. By then he owned a scrap-metal yard and introduced Elza to Morris Kamin, who worked for him as an office boy. It was the only job he would ever hold, for forty-four years. Aladar had always said to him: "That's not a job for a fine young man like you," but Morris ignored the remark. He disliked any form of pressure, which made soft-spoken Elza his ideal mate. She rarely left the house except for shopping and synagogue, or to visit her brother's family. But Morris's relatives found her quiet manner unnerving, and their visits became infrequent.

Once her daughters entered school, Elza began helping neighbors with dress alterations. Over the years a group of women — "my regulars," she'd call them — brought her enough dresses and skirts and, as fashions changed, slacks, to keep two women occupied. Elza never complained, but she never seemed to hurry either, and when Aladar suggested that she get a job with one of the downtown department stores ("This is piecework — an employer would at least pay you benefits") she said, smiling, "Oh, I wouldn't like that." During Rosie's last year of university, Elza committed suicide with an overdose of Seconal. No one knew how she got the pills, no one guessed she'd gone to a doctor with complaints about her nerves.

Rosie tried to read herself out of mourning. Working part-time in the library on campus, she knew where to find the volumes about Holocaust survivors and their children. And the books on suicide too. None of them helped, but she read each one to the end. Perhaps she hadn't really expected much from them: yes, it was true, people suffered. She hadn't needed books to figure that out.

After Elza's death Rosie avoided any thought of the future with laundry, ironing, shopping, cleaning. This happened during the Vietnam years, when she was on the edge of campus protests and often filled with dread. Deb had just gone away to Penn State, and claimed that the long bus ride made visits home inconvenient. Rosie was left with Morris, who had never taken care of himself.

At first she tried to re-create her mother's meals, boiling tongue or frying tuna patties, while her father impatiently read the evening paper. Over dinner he would lecture her about the price of food. Why did he have to talk with his mouth full? She watched him chew. He never commented on her meals. Aunt Pearl, Uncle Aladar's wife, had offered to teach her "the secrets of the Jewish kitchen," as she called them. "You have to feed your father right. It's what your mother would want." Rosie declined the offer.

She went directly from her political science lectures to the A&P, like a woman married twenty-five years, hurrying past young hand-holding couples in suede vests, blue jeans and beaded headbands. Inside the shops and bars they drank beer, rolled joints, talked about sex, listened to Dylan. Rosie had to be home in time to feed her father.

"How's Daddy?" Deb would ask when she called on Sundays. "How *is* your father?" Uncle Aladar asked, checking in. "What are you cooking for your father's dinner?" asked Aunt Pearl, reminding Rosie that the A&P had a special on brisket. Answering mechanically, she slumped at the kitchen table, holding the phone away from her ear. Why did her mother take the pills?

"Your father always said I make the best latkes," Pearl tempted. "I could teach you."

After dinner, most evenings, she took the bus back to campus and found an isolated place in the library where she could read. She wanted to be at home in her room, but Morris might interrupt ("When you washed this shirt you lost another button") and end with a lecture on all the money she spent for food. In the library, she might put her books aside and sleep. She knew it would be possible to sleep for days on end.

Why did her mother take the pills?

Rosie sifted through memories. Once she had discussed a dream with Elza, who listened intently as she sewed. Two nights in a row she'd wakened from a pool of green water where soldiers bathed after battle. Suddenly, before the men could finish, they were running for cover and turning into some drawing she'd seen in an art book: naked soldiers bathing, their limbs exaggerated, heroic.

"I can explain that," Elza had said, relying on common sense and tales from her grandmother, while Rosie used Jung. Elza, surprised to find they had symbols in common, asked if Jung had been born in Hungary. Laughing, Rosie answered, "That isn't how the unconscious works, Ma, it's not only Hungarian. Or Jewish."

"Tell me about this unconscious," Elza asked.

Rosie strung together a few ideas that seemed hopelessly vague.

"Then it's like the soul," Elza concluded, so pleased with herself that Rosie stopped short of saying "not exactly."

Did her mother believe in the soul? Rosie wondered. Did she think there was life after death?

Using her mother's pots and pans, or mop and pail, or needles and thread, Rosie felt no closer to the woman who had stuffed herself with pills. She remembered being four-teen, possibly fifteen, reading in her bedroom. It was a hot summer evening and she'd taken off her top and bra. Even then Rosie had heavy large breasts that embarrassed her, and from reading D. H. Lawrence she'd gotten the notion of making friends with her body. Her mother knocked on the door and Rosie called for her to come in. When she did, a look of horror crossed her face. "Can't you keep your clothes on?" Elza had whispered, retreating into the hall-way. "What would your father think?"

Now Rosie could have answered: "As long as he's fed on time, he wouldn't notice." She knew this to be untrue, but preferred to think it. Deb, who was studying psychol-ogy, said that he'd run their mother into the ground. "Did he ever notice her?" she asked bitterly. Rosie thought so. Hadn't they loved each other? But if they had, why the pills?

In the spring of her graduating year, six months after Elza's funeral, Rosie was raped. She blamed herself and never mentioned the incident that had begun in the library one evening, where a black graduate student she often saw there was studying at a nearby table. Occasionally they'd nodded — he seemed pleasant and even familiar, perhaps they'd been in a lecture course together, or at a rally, she couldn't remember which — and in the elevator he'd asked if she wanted to stop somewhere for coffee. Rosie agreed eagerly: it was April and the campus smelled of lilacs. Even when he suggested going back to his place, she agreed. It was that kind of night. As soon as they entered his room she felt his hands everywhere. "Just do this," he'd said, his mouth smashing against hers. His people had suffered terribly, been enslaved. What right did she have to say no? She pushed him away, but he was stronger. It was her first encounter with sex.

Over dinner the next day Rosie wondered why her father couldn't see a difference in her. She'd always envied the girls at school who claimed to have gotten rid of their virginity by eighteen so they could look a man straight in the eye. Morris slurped his soup — canned: there were limits to what she would cook — while Rosie contemplated telling him about the previous evening. Maybe Deb was right.

Rosie thought of joining several antiwar marches, especially one to Washington, but the timing was always wrong.

When she graduated in June, all the choices before her seemed remote. She needed several more courses for a teaching certificate, having ignored the dull requirements of an education degree, but debated about library school or getting a master's. "You don't need a regular job," Morris told her, "stay at home and take care of the house." Nothing in his voice suggested he saw an alternative. Deb was planning to spend the summer on campus, where she'd found a temporary job waitressing. "Dad's used to you," she explained over the telephone. Rosie felt a tightness in her chest.

She kept her part-time job at the library, moving up from shelving books to the circulation desk, twenty hours a week. Though she never admitted it, Rosie had preferred shelving: it was more satisfying to put things in order than to watch the titles flow in and out, like waves on a beach. And you didn't need to bother with people.

Uncle Aladar gave her a check for one hundred dollars as a graduation present and suggested that she save it toward a ticket to Europe: "You should travel a bit before you get married. After studying French all these years, why not go to Paris?" *Get married?* Had she misunderstood him? "You could go for a few weeks in the fall. Nice weather then."

Aunt Pearl called with the news that there was a new folk-dancing club at the synagogue. "And not only for the Young Marrieds," she enthused.

Why did her mother take the pills?

Summer passed, fall came and went. Gradually friends from college called less often, getting on with their lives. Rosie's body ached. Tuesday: fried fish. Wednesday: brisket. Thursday: leftovers. Friday: boiled chicken. She even lit the Sabbath candles at the end of each week as her mother had done. All those girls in the library with long, flowing hair. Did it really matter if she washed hers? She twisted it into a dirty coil, ate too many Fig Newtons, thumbed through her old textbooks. Winter was passing.

"The best years of your life," Aunt Pearl warned. "You'll never be this free again." There was a young man at synagogue, 4-F, they said — she could find out more.

Rosie would stand in front of the shelves of cookies at the A&P, trying to choose between Oreos and Fig Newtons. She had gained fifteen pounds.

At the library she asked for additional hours, but there wasn't enough work to justify them. Perhaps next summer, her supervisor offered. Had she decided yet on library school? Rosie was evasive.

"But you already work in the library," Morris said that evening. "You could probably teach them a thing or two." She tried to explain the difference but he barely listened, while Walter Cronkite's voice droned on about Vietnam. "It's enough school already — just take care of the house. And let me watch the news."

"Listen to your father," Aunt Pearl suggested. Rosie guessed that he had been complaining to Uncle Aladar, who'd asked his wife to intervene. "He knows what's best for you."

"This is 1970, Auntie. Not some old-country ghetto."

"Now you sound like my Joel."

Rosie had always disliked her robust cousin, a law student who still complained that he'd missed the '67 war in Israel. But sons, at least, could speak up for themselves. Uncle Aladar had raised his own daughters to accept their feminine nature: eagerness tempered by docility.

For the first time Rosie understood that Elza had been her ally. As she went through her mother's sewing box, preparing to let out a skirt, she remembered their quarrels and wondered if her mother had known how much she loved her. Rosie had never been interested in sewing, embroidering, crocheting — always claiming that she had no talent for them — and now she found that she couldn't even repair the waistband of her favorite black skirt. With a seamstress for a mother, she hardly knew how to change a button. Overcome with regret, she tossed the skirt into the back of her closet and went shopping for a new one. That night, after feeding Morris, she ate herself sick on Oreos.

Two weeks later her father came down with the flu, and then Rosie took to her bed. But each afternoon she went into the kitchen and prepared Morris's meal. When the rich, sweet scent of pan-roasted carrots made her gag, she opened the kitchen door for fresh air. Looking out into the backyard Rosie noticed that the forsythia had opened, bright yellow flowers spotting the grim March day. Her mother had always cut some for the crystal vase kept in the middle of the dining room table. "We had these in Budapest, when I was a girl," her mother once said. Or am I imagining that, Rosie wondered? She might ask Deb, who would be annoyed at the question.

"You should eat, to keep up your strength," Morris cautioned, waiting for her to serve him. "But I'm not hungry," Rosie replied. "I can't keep anything down." She drank pots of tea, ate Saltines.

She continued sifting memories. Why had her family never been on a vacation? Other people went to the beach, sat in the sun, burned themselves happily. For a moment Rosie even forgot that she was one of the few graduates of Nathan Hale High who hadn't learned to swim, though her pathetic splashings had been passed by a generous teacher. Rosie imagined a beach: Water lapping. Sunshine. In the summer, to keep cool, her mother had sewed in the basement, listening to Arthur Godfrey on the radio. How is it, Rosie thought, that we managed to have running water in the house? Why not a well behind the garage? At night she slept with one hand between her legs.

As soon as Rosie recovered, Morris cut back the weekly grocery allowance. "You're putting on weight," he said accusingly, and she knew what he meant: with every new pound she took another step back from a husband, that creature as mythical as a unicorn. She weighed herself and, even after the flu, had gained six more pounds.

Aunt Pearl telephoned. "Aladar and me, we're taking the children to Israel in August. A real family vacation. And

Aladar wants you to come along. He told me to ask you, his sister's daughter. It won't cost you a penny, nothing, all you have to do is lose twenty pounds. That's easy. And you'll get to see Israel."

Was there a beach at the Dead Sea?

Why did her mother take the pills?

Rosie telephoned her uncle to thank him for the offer. However Israel was the last place on earth she wanted to visit. "About my mother," she began, tentatively. "The poor woman's dead," he interrupted. "Let her rest in peace." He rambled on. There was plenty of time to lose twenty pounds before August. Just five pounds a month. Anyone could do it with enough cottage cheese. Talk to her aunt.

"Why," Morris asked, more frequently now, "do you have to leave wet stockings hanging by the shower curtain? Your mother never did that." Embarrassed, Rosie told herself to wash them in the basement. "Why do you have to leave crumbs on the table, dust balls under the bed, used cups in the sink?" Rosie promised to do better. "Why . . ." he began, ready to pounce, and Rosie said, "I know, I know, whatever it is, my mother never did that." "Shut your mouth!" Morris shouted, his face darkening red. Beet red, Rosie thought. Like a bowl of borscht. She tried not to laugh. "Ungrateful girl! I want you to start coming to synagogue."

Since she was fifteen Rosie hadn't gone to synagogue with her parents, and she had no intention of starting now. So she lied, claiming she had been able to get some extra hours at the library.

Temporarily placated, Morris reminded her that Uncle Aladar expected them for passover seder on Tuesday night. "But you know I have to work then" — another lie — "part-timers always get the worst hours."

Instead of joining her family, she ate supper alone in the Student Union and went to a movie in the campus's French film series. *Jules et Jim*. The heroine, poor, pouty Jeanne Moreau, had to drive off a bridge to be free of her men. But that was in the 1930s — today she could have taken a handful of Seconals.

Rosie began buying TV dinners for her father and spending more nights on campus. "I have to work," she explained. "It's the end of the semester. Some of the other part-timers are busy with exams." This lie came out so smoothly she had to admire it.

Then one evening at the film series Rosie saw the black graduate student in the audience, holding hands with the blondest blonde around. Such delicate long hair, no doubt smelling like a garden, and bell-bottomed jeans embroidered with flowers. She almost felt envious, and the thought frightened her.

Rosie looked around the audience, aware that she was the only woman there wearing polyester slacks that stretched comfortably at the waist. She tried to remember her body a year or two years back. Even though she wore large silver earrings with turquoise beads, earrings that might be the envy of anyone in the audience, she still had on maroon polyester stretch pants.

The next morning, almost a year to the day after her graduation, she went to the travel agent near campus and bought a round-trip ticket to Paris. The student rates were so reasonable, she later told Morris, that she couldn't resist. This, too, was a lie, although the fare had in fact been a good one. But Rosie didn't care about the price. She had enough money in her bank account to stake her for six months while she found work. And then there was her return ticket. Once she got to Paris she would cash it in.

3

SEVERAL DAYS AFTER Rosie had begun her affair with Serge she felt her first doubts. Although he seemed to understand her moods better than any man she'd known (or maybe, she thought, he ignored them), the doubts lingered and grew. Accustomed to waiting for a man's telephone call, to wondering if he would call, and when, and what it might mean, Rosie had little experience predicting the next step. Three months passed before she started to enjoy her new situation, yet even then the affair seemed incomplete, as if it were happening to a colleague at work, something she had to comment on, even encourage: "Of course you should keep seeing him." Words like that.

Well into the first year of living with him she continued to distrust whatever had brought them together. Her body, he liked to say, was a map of America. Visits to his mother's village, evenings with his friends, walks around unfamiliar neighborhoods — walks that reminded her of her first months in Paris, when she'd been overcome by a desire to possess it all, as if the city could be possessed only by walking, by seeing every corner — changed nothing. Serge would point out museums, cafés, famous brothels, or take her into wonderful bookstores, and while she stood amazed that after ten years she hadn't known of each place before, Rosie dismissed the notion that ahead were days to discover the unexpected. Then one evening, sitting on a bench in Luxembourg Gardens, Rosie saw that she had come to trust Serge. They'd been debating the merits of different routes home — the sort of discussion she thrived on. Although they both knew his choice to be the more interesting one, he relented, shrugged happily and said, "Oh well, we'll see that some other time." At that moment Rosie decided she loved him.

Serge was older than her by twelve years, and only an inch or two taller, a plain, unassuming man, bone-thin. His large ears seemed all the more prominent because he was balding; unlike the rest of his thinning brown hair, his side-burns were gray. He dressed in unfashionable clothes, and his eyesight was so poor that he could almost claim to be legally blind. Because of this he had changed jobs frequently, to find one he could do without relying on his sight. For the last three years he'd worked as a ticket-taker in a small repertory cinema in the Latin Quarter, often saying that on any given night there were more movies showing in Paris than in any other city in the world. "How can you know?" Rosie always asked. "Everyone does," Serge would reply. Sundays, he frequently gave his time to selling the Communist newspaper *L'Humanité* in front of a café near their street. The daily *Humanité* was available at newsstands, but on Sundays party members sold it themselves.

Rosie had planned to be alone with Serge on the night of his return from the hospital, where he had been admitted for tests, after several weeks of abdominal cramps. His best friends, Renée and Thierry Roussel, also party members, had visited there daily, bringing the latest gossip, but she had hoped they would have enough sense to let him rest after dropping him off. She should have known better. Of course Serge invited them up, it wasn't in his nature to think of his health first, or to think of himself without people around. There was no wine in the house, and he tried to hide his disappointment.

"You really have to cut back," Renée said. She had tied a large red silk scarf around her head, like a turban. Rosie admired her flair. Renée had found her style at a young age and now worked only to maintain it. For the last ten years she'd been writing film reviews for *L'Humanité* while completing a book about the politics of French films between the wars.

"I never knew you thought much of doctors," he said.

Rosie thought that she had missed something. "Why shouldn't he have a drink?" she asked.

"Darling," Renée said, lighting a Gitane, "the liver is a fragile organ. And you can't live without one. It takes a lot of abuse but then one day, well, that's it."

"Don't frighten Rosie," Serge said. "And what about your cigarettes? Lungs are fragile too."

"No wine, no cigarettes, what's to become of us?" Thierry asked, laughing. His clothes and beard were uncared for, even graceless, suggesting a romantic idealism — like that of his strong features — which belied a man of moderation. "I suppose we have to give up coffee too, and salt, and . . ."

"We don't have to get fanatical about it," Renée said. "I'm not talking about religion, but really, Serge . . ."

"My father drank at least a litre of red wine a day."

"So did mine," Thierry added. A friend of Serge's since boyhood, after high school he had taken a job as a typesetter and become active in the printers' union, which had consumed his life.

"That doesn't mean a thing. It's a well-known fact that most Frenchmen are drunks."

Rosie never knew what to say when Renée spoke like that. If Rosie had generalized about the French, Renée would have corrected her and gone on to say something more outrageous herself.

"You're sure there's nothing in the house?" Serge asked. "The one thing that kept me alive in the hospital was the thought of a glass of wine."

"Isn't it enough to be home?" Thierry asked, and Rosie suddenly thought that he was taking her side, although sides hadn't exactly been drawn.

"You're right," Serge said. "It's enough. I could barely sleep, and the food . . ."

"Ah, we're back to the pleasures of the senses," Renée said, stubbing out her cigarette and immediately lighting another.

"And I kept worrying about Rosie."

"About me? I can take care of myself."

"I know that."

"You two probably want to be alone," Renée said. "If I know Serge."

Rosie frowned. Fifteen years ago he and Renée had slept together a few times — "For company," he'd always said — but Renée still acted as if she owned a secret piece of Serge, even though she and Thierry had been married for more than a decade. Renée even claimed that she could only love a man with drive, with ambition, and said this often enough in front of Serge for Rosie to be embarrassed, though he never seemed to mind. Thierry, she believed, had also accepted Renée's notions, yet no one could call him ambitious. Maybe this is what happened to people when they turned fifty: how fine it must be, to want what you had.

"We probably shouldn't have come up," Renée went on, but she made no move to go.

"Don't say that," Serge replied.

"We're going now." Thierry stood up. "You should be resting."

"Is that what the doctor said?" Rosie asked.

"They never say anything useful, just enough to keep you coming back so they can get rich."

"I won't disagree with that," Renée said, dropping a cigarette lighter into her purse.

Rosie noticed that her red fingernail polish was chipped, but somehow on Renée it seemed almost chic, as if no reasonable woman gave her fingernails much attention. "But you think Serge is all right?" Rosie asked.

"Of course he is," Renée said, crossing the room to kiss him on the cheeks. She carried herself as if she were in a movie.

"Why don't the two of you go away for the weekend?" Thierry suggested.

"Yes, a weekend in the country," Renée added.

"We'll think about it." Serge embraced his friends and saw them to the door while Rosie took the ashtray, full of Renée's butts, and emptied it in the kitchen wastebasket.

"Would you like to go away?" She called to him cheerfully. "It's a good idea."

"I'm still a little tired."

"We could visit your mother." Serge's family lived in a small village several hours from the city.

"We could."

"Or we could go to Giverny. It's closer."

"That would be nice too."

Once a year Rosie and Serge took the train to Giverny and visited Monet's garden, often saying that sometime they must spend a night in the village. Neither admitted that they went mainly because it was just an hour's ride. In fact Serge had always disliked the Impressionists ("those pink bourgeois"), and preferred the countryside to any planned garden.

"You'd probably rather visit your mother."

"Don't listen to everything Renée says. She's not always right."

Rosie walked into the living room. "If you don't want to go . . ." she began.

"I have no patience," he apologized. "I just need to rest." Serge motioned her to sit beside him on the sofa. "I want to ask you something," he said.

"What can I get you?"

"I don't need anything, Rosie. I want to talk."

She was tempted to lean against him, but didn't. "What's wrong?" In the hospital she'd never been able to ask, but now the question came out effortlessly.

"Two days ago I had a visitor."

"Yes."

"Someone you know."

She closed her eyes for an instant. Serge's voice was gentle.

"Benyoub."

"The bastard!" she exclaimed.

"Why say that?"

"Oh Serge . . ."

"I mean it, Rosie."

"He had no business . . ."

"When people are desperate . . ."

"He's always desperate."

"You dislike him that much?"

"It's not a question of liking or disliking. What did he tell you?"

"That he'd been to see you, to borrow money. And that you said it wasn't your decision alone . . ."

"I never said that."

"What did you say?"

"I don't remember exactly, but I didn't encourage him, I suggested he ask his cousin . . ."

"Hamed?"

"He brought up Hamed too?" Rosie felt her hands like heavy weights. "Why did you listen?"

As soon as she had asked the question, Rosie knew how foolish it sounded. Serge couldn't resist a request for help: he was always chasing after some neighbor, going along to a government office to sort out a problem, buying medicine, running errands. People sought Serge out to offer him problems.

"He surprised me," Serge said.

"It wasn't my idea. When did he come?"

"I'm not accusing you."

"I never thought he'd bother you in the hospital."

"He was very polite. He came into the ward and introduced himself and said he didn't mean to disturb me. I could hardly refuse to listen, he looked so sad. And he was very well-spoken. Sincere."

"Sincere!" Rosie snorted.

"He said how much you'd meant to him, and that he wished you could be friends. 'After living with someone for five years, at least you should be friends' — I think that's how he put it. And you know, I agree with him."

Rosie sighed. The way men saw the world! And they thought women were sentimental. "Then he mentioned the money?"

"He said you told him to ask Hamed."

Rosie bristled. Hamed was a sore point between her and the world.

Serge put his arm around Rosie's shoulders, and she leaned against him. He smelled of hospital soap. She rested one hand on his thigh. "I missed you so much," she said.

Rosie had been living with Hamed off and on for two years when she met Benyoub. She preferred not to remember this time in her life. Deb used to ask what she thought she was doing — sleeping with the entire Third World? Now Rosie thought that Deb's remarks were part of the reason she stayed with Hamed as long as she did.

Like Benyoub, Hamed needed a woman to take care of him, but he lacked Ben's virtues. He lied easily, slept with anyone he wanted, and turned her apartment into a half-way house for illegal immigrants from Algeria — there always seemed to be several strangers asleep on the floor of the cramped living room. When she complained, Hamed said it was typical French selfishness to be bothered by them. "But I'm not even French," Rosie used to argue, yet she already knew his answer: "French, American, you think there's a difference?" He had been a student too, claiming that ethno-musicology could unite people, if only they would learn to listen to each other. (This Rosie had found sensible.) After a year together she became pregnant, and when he demanded an abortion, she agreed. Somehow, he promised, he would pay for half of it; then he vanished for a month.

Rosie had few qualms about an abortion, being numb at the time, but later she regretted that her only pregnancy had been with Hamed. Benyoub insisted on birth control, and Serge believed there were already too many children in the world. Sometimes Rosie wondered whether her baby would have been a boy or a girl. And every year, on August 10, she remembered the abortion. She had never told Deb, but Benyoub knew, and of course Serge.

"What did he say?" Rosie asked.

Serge pulled her closer. "That maybe we could help a little."

"But he wants twenty thousand francs."

"Well, we can't give him that. But we owe him something. The way that bastard Le Pen goes on about immigration . . ."

"No, no, we can't. I wonder if he'll go to Hamed." She hoped that Serge wouldn't start up about Le Pen and the National Front. It couldn't be good for him to become excited, even if he was right.

Serge stroked her head. "Your hair feels thicker, I think the new treatment's working."

"I hope so — it costs enough. Did I tell you I have to get my head massaged twice a week?"

"I could learn how."

She liked the way his hand caressed her head. She felt safe. "Did you get Ben to tell you what his problem is?"

"I didn't like to ask. That's his business. And he didn't ask for help with a problem. He knows what he needs — money."

"Still, I wonder what he needs it for."

"He's working?"

"I think so. If he's telling the truth. He used to send money home to his family. He has a wife in Algeria."

"You never mentioned that before."

"I must have," Rosie said, guessing that she had avoided the subject. "That shows how much you listen to me."

"I listen to you, Rosie."

"It wasn't a real marriage. His mother arranged it when he was sixteen, so the girl could move in with his family and help with the chores. They never loved each other, and Karima always knew he wanted to divorce her. I think that's one of the reasons he came to Paris, for a life of his own. The mother is something else, a real ayatollah."

"You think the money's for her?"

"With Ben, anything's possible. But you know it'll take forever to get him to pay it back, it's really more of a gift. We can't count on him."

"We have to do something."

Rosie wanted to ask why, but resisted. It bothered her that sharp words rolled off her tongue so easily, that she often felt annoyed with people. "I guess I'm just being paranoid. Once burned, twice shy — you know all that." For the past year, since Serge hadn't been able to work, Rosie had paid all the bills. She disliked talking about money with him, which left her dissatisfied with herself. She was younger than Serge, and stronger, and work came more easily to her.

"Let's not talk about him any more tonight," she said. "I'm so glad you're home."

"I've been looking forward to sleeping in my own bed. Tomorrow I may sleep all day."

"You should."

"And I want to wash off the hospital stench. I can still smell it on my skin."

"While you shower, I'll put fresh sheets on the bed."

Serge disentangled himself from her slowly. "Good. Especially if you'll keep me company."

"You don't have a choice."

In their bedroom Rosie took out her favorite sheets, a pale sage green, and removed the Mexican blanket she used as a bedspread. A square of heavy old lace over the bedside lampshade gave the light a soft glow, as if it were polished. Serge's record collection covered half of the burled walnut buffet beside Rosie's reproductions of pre-Colombian statues and the tarnished silver picture frames she'd found at the Clignancourt flea market.

Tucking the edge of a sheet under the mattress, Rosie enjoyed the sound of the running shower: it meant Serge was home. She felt ashamed about Benyoub's visit to him and wanted to forget it. Ben had a way of making her feel responsible for his behavior. Idiotic, but there it was. Long ago she had tired of feeling shame on his account, so the intensity of her emotions tonight surprised her.

Shame, she reflected, is useless, a waste of energy. And she knew Serge agreed. He called it a Catholic specialty but she didn't think Catholics had a monopoly. "You're confusing shame with guilt," he'd said. "For Catholics it's shame, for Jews it's guilt." They could talk for hours about the differences.

But not tonight. Rosie smoothed the sheet flat. It felt cool to touch and had a slight scent of lavender, picked up from a sachet. She'd meant to vacuum the rug that afternoon. Serge's clothes were always rumpled, but he liked the apartment to be clean. Rosie rarely noticed dust. Serge had left the bathroom door open and she stood watching as he dried himself. Despite his stay in the hospital, he looked thinner than ever. Why hadn't the doctors helped? Then he turned away, and Rosie guessed that he knew she was watching him. Serge's modesty still surprised her, for he was a good lover. Benyoub would have basked in her attention, even toweled himself more slowly, or invited her to dry his back.

"Can I get anything for you?" she asked, plumping the pillows.

"Come to bed with me now," he said.

Without answering, Rosie began to undress, tossing her clothes on a wicker chair in the corner. They hadn't touched each other for over a month. Naked, finally, she hurried into the living room and switched off the light. A slight breeze came in from the street.

Serge was standing by the bed when she returned and encircled his waist with her arms, looking straight into his eyes. Quickly he pulled her around, and, standing behind her, caressed her breasts. Her nipples stiffened as she felt him grow hard against her buttocks.

"Did you miss me very much?" she asked.

His tongue moved across the back of her neck, toward her left shoulder, until he closed his mouth on it. She could feel his teeth biting gently. Was he being kind when he'd said that the new hair treatments were working? One hand continued to caress her breast, the other stroked her stomach and gradually settled between her legs. She watched the hands, almost disembodied. His wrist bones looked sharp.

"Of course I missed you," he replied, pushing her down on the bed, their legs entwined.

Rosie felt his erection press into the cleft of her buttocks. She took a deep breath.

"I missed you too much."

4

ROSIE FOUND HERSELF waiting for a telephone call from Benyoub. At work she expected a message, at home she knew the phone would ring soon. And the familiar sensation of waiting stirred her memories. Life in Paris seemed to break into three stages: before Ben, with him, and after, like one of the murky old triptychs in the Louvre. Why, she wondered, was it impossible to will herself out of an emotion she didn't want to feel?

She sat quietly beside Serge in the living room, trying to read but instead remembering the past twenty years. She could see whole afternoons, entire days: an argument in a restaurant, a vacation in the Dordogne, people she hadn't thought of in years. Life was not allegorical. Her open briefcase, beside her on the sofa, was stuffed with students' papers full of spelling mistakes and hopeless verbs.

Her first job in Paris had lasted a month. Through the *Herald Tribune* she'd learned of a couple seeking an au pair who spoke English, and although children confused her, Rosie moved into the Aubrets' large apartment on boulevard Raspail. She had enjoyed their impressive library, and also liked the record collection, which surprisingly included

Odetta and Buffy St. Marie. And she'd liked Bernard Aubret. His tight-lipped English wife Hilary, and their two-year-old son Leon, who took after his mother, were another matter. Hilary had explained that she wanted Rosie to over-see Leon's toilet training — "a very very important respon-sibility," as she'd put it. Hilary worked for the British Embassy; Bernard taught at the Sorbonne. What had hap-pened to them?

Every morning Rosie had spread newspaper on the Oriental rug in their living room and set out a plastic potty, which she thought resembled a miniature electric chair, strapped Leon to it, put some Miles Davis on the stereo (Rosie was acquainting herself with American jazz) and told the crying boy it was time to make do-do. "Don't you like music?" she would say later, staring into the empty pot. When Bernard had invited her into the study one evening and almost sheepishly explained his wife's concern about Leon's lack of progress, Rosie wanted to put her arms around him. Instead she gave two weeks' notice. She hadn't come all the way to Paris for this. But while living with the Aubrets Rosie had begun dieting, and she had her hair cut in a short, waiflike style that she never changed. Paris seemed to bring out a certain flair in her, and she went along with it, feeling European. When frightened or de-pressed, Rosie reminded herself that she was living in Paris. What would her mother have thought of that?

Rosie's next job, teaching English at the Continental Language School, made her feel that she was becoming part of the city. At first she considered the simple, repeti-tive lessons as good as shelving books in the library back home. And the English division of Continental was a mecca for people who wanted to leave families and coun-tries behind them. Rosie was quickly befriended by her col-leagues, a Hungarian lesbian who claimed to be a countess, an Irish spinster, and a draft dodger from Milwaukee who warned her to stay away from American graduate students in Paris.

Over the years Rosie grew restless repeating the same questions, coaxing the same replies, and occasionally told herself to look for other work. But Continental was safe. In time she had more seniority than any other teacher, puzzling her supervisors, who were accustomed to a turnover that kept salaries low. After they understood that Rosie had no interest in administration (jobs always filled by the French in any case), she was moved to the head office and given more important students — government officials or minor movie stars with an eye on America. Yet she preferred her older students, usually widows overcome with a desire to learn English.

"Where are you?" Serge asked, looking up from his newspaper.

Rosie shrugged. "Just thinking."

"We don't have to loan him anything," he said.

"How did you know I was thinking about Benyoub?"

"A safe guess."

"What do you mean?"

"I know what you're feeling. These situations are never clear. We don't have to lend him a franc."

"But you offered."

"People change their minds."

"You're only saying that because you think it's what I want to hear." She knew Serge was right: if Benyoub phoned, she should just give him the money. He might not even call.

"It's not important enough to worry about," he said.

But worrying, fussing, running her mind over slights and recriminations, had become Rosie's way. "I feel like such a small person," she said.

"He's not that important."

"You'd give him the money, you wouldn't think twice. I'd like to be that way too."

"I never lived with him."

"That doesn't matter and you know it. I'm not generous the way you are."

"You're generous in a different way, Rosie."

"You're just saying that to please me. I know."

Serge shook his head. "You won't listen, will you?"

"I'm listening."

"You'd stop all this fussing if you listened. There isn't one way of doing things, only one way that's right. Benyoub was probably wrong to ask you for help, but apparently he didn't think he had a choice."

"You sound like a philosophy professor."

Serge smiled. "But that's what it takes to live with you."

Rosie looked away from him.

"And don't start pouting. Let's go out instead. I want to stop by the newspaper office and then we can have a drink. It'll get your mind off yourself a lot faster than sitting around here while I reassure you that you're wonderful and I love you."

Despite her mood Rosie laughed. "I suppose we could go out."

The telephone rang, and they looked at each other.

"We don't have to answer it," Serge said.

"No. We don't."

She picked up the receiver. "Hello." She paused, and then, "I don't know." Her voice sounded casual.

Serge leaned forward.

"Yes, yes, we'll help." She nodded at him, and their eyes locked. "Of course I'll meet you."

Serge leaned back, watching her.

"Tonight's okay, if you're in a hurry. You know where I live."

She put down the receiver but didn't immediately remove her hand from the telephone. "He asked if you'd be here. He said he liked you."

"Do you want me to stay?"

"I don't know what I want."

Serge laughed. "I knew you'd say that."

"Then you're staying?"

He nodded. "Why not? We can go out after he leaves."

"You should be getting your rest. I hope this isn't upsetting you. You must think I'm pretty selfish."

"When is he coming, Rosie?"

"At nine."

"We should offer him a drink. Maybe some wine."

"I didn't buy any."

"I bought some today."

"But you're not supposed to be drinking now."

"Who told you that? I'm supposed to cut back, that's all."

Serge had been home for only two days and Rosie wanted the right moment to talk about his health. Dreading even the prospect of Benyoub's visit, she decided this wasn't it. "I won't argue with you tonight."

"There's nothing to argue about. We'll all have some wine."

"Ben never drank much. I don't think Muslims do. It's forbidden or something."

"He's very handsome," Serge said. "Almost beautiful. I don't think you mentioned that."

"I showed you his picture."

"I don't remember."

My Arab prince, she used to call him. With dark, almond-shaped eyes, like someone out of an illustrated edition of the *Arabian Nights* she vaguely recalled borrowing from her elementary-school library a hundred years ago.

"I'm sure I did."

My Jewish princess, Benyoub would whisper back, but she'd always said: "Oh, don't call me that." Since he rarely used endearments, she never had the heart to explain why it sounded like an insult.

"I'd like some wine," Serge said, heading toward the kitchen. "Want a glass?"

"No," Rosie called after him. These days, red wine either gave her a headache or left her feeling queasy. With each year the list of things she couldn't eat or drink without getting an upset stomach had increased, from heavy cream to fried foods. So this was forty. The middle-aged joggers on the canal could try to beat it for a while, but in medieval times they would have been old, if not already dead. Rosie smiled.

When Benyoub arrived half an hour early Rosie wondered if he had telephoned from a nearby café, ready to visit if she invited him over. Suspicion, she thought, had become another of her moral failings.

"This is Serge," she said, introducing the two men as she gestured Benyoub to a chair. Then she flinched: "But you've already met."

Benyoub was wearing a crisply ironed white shirt. There's a decent laundry wherever he lives, Rosie thought.

Serge offered wine and Benyoub accepted, though without much interest, she felt. He seemed to be watching her and Serge, trying to gauge their reaction to him. The comfortable childless couple? Did that run through his mind? He had rolled his shirt sleeves to his elbows and she noticed the watch on his left wrist. It looked expensive.

"It's very kind of you to ask me here," Benyoub said.

No one replied so they listened as Serge took a sip of his wine.

"On my way over I remembered the time you came with me to Algeria."

Please not that, thought Rosie.

"What year?" Serge asked.

"It was '79, wasn't it?" Benyoub turned to Rosie.

Did he feel contempt for her? She looked into his face.

"You thought the country was beautiful."

"Did I?"

He nodded.

"I'm sorry, I don't remember."

"You should, it's very beautiful."

Rosie wished she hadn't lied. Benyoub still seemed overwhelmed by an awareness of the ease with which he could be hurt. His family lived in a rambling old house that seemed only half inhabited, and she had loved its Islamic arches, which sloped as gently as human flesh, and the rough wooden lattices over windows cut high into the walls. She could remember the sound of her footsteps on the ceramic tiles that covered the courtyard.

"I was in Algeria. With the army, in 1960," Serge said. "During the revolution."

"I remember the poverty," Rosie said, immediately wishing she could take back the words. "I mean the people were so poor, it made me angry."

"Thanks to the French," Benyoub said, and then looked at Serge.

"The French, yes, we certainly didn't help. But it's more than a matter of nations." Serge often said it was Algeria that had made him a Communist, more by sympathy than conviction; he had little use for polemics.

"Nations?" Benyoub's voice rose slightly.

"Imperialism is a stage in the development of nations, but it's more than that. Think of . . ."

The development of nations. Serge had found his element, Rosie thought. What had he and Ben talked about in the hospital? Dialectical materialism? She could force herself to sit back and enjoy their exchange, like an ordinary evening's visit with friends, but the idea struck her as insane. She wanted to laugh, and for no reason that she could explain, felt Ben was aware of this.

As the two men talked, Rosie tried to list the things they had in common. People always said you kept falling in love with the same person over and over again, but she didn't agree. There couldn't be two men more different than Benyoub and Serge. Except that they both liked anal sex, which she'd gone along with although it had never appealed to her. The Muslim boy and the Catholic boy, having once enjoyed this way of avoiding pregnancies, still remained attached to it. They had that in common. Did it remind them of their youth? One afternoon in the Continental lunch room several of the women teachers had started talking about anal sex. Rosie hadn't confided in them, and now couldn't remember exactly what had been said, except for a young Polish teacher admitting that she'd practiced with a candle in order to please her boyfriend. The image remained with Rosie, and never failed to make her sad. It seemed a key to the gulf between men and women.

"And how is your sister?" Benyoub was asking. Apparently he and Serge had found some common ground.

"She's coming to visit next week. She just won a trip to Paris for two."

"Won?"

"She enters contests. As a hobby. It's very American," Rosie said lightly. "All kinds of companies use them as advertising gimmicks."

Benyoub looked baffled.

"She's won a trip to London, several cruises in the Caribbean, and endless microwaves and golf clubs and televisions — things like that." Deb had once sent her the list of prizes she'd collected and Rosie enjoyed telling friends about them, watching their expressions change from interest to amusement to something like horror. She understood how they felt.

"Who's she bringing to Paris?"

"I don't know — it's best to wait until she tells me. Long ago I learned never to ask her questions. She always thinks I'm prying."

Deb had disliked Benyoub on sight. "How could you go with an Arab?" she'd said. That night Benyoub had asked, "Why does she wear such a dirty raincoat?" Fortunately Deb only visited Europe when she won a plane ticket.

"She's an unhappy girl," said Serge.

"You only met once," Rosie said.

Benyoub had barely touched his wine, and he set the glass on a table beside him. "You must give her my regards."

"Yes, of course."

He looked as if he were about to say something more, but then thought otherwise.

"She's learning Yiddish now," Rosie added. "But we never spoke it at home." Why, she wondered, am I telling him this? "Apparently it's the thing with a certain group in America."

"Didn't your mother speak Yiddish?" Serge asked.

"I don't know. At least not to me. But she was from Budapest. I read somewhere that the Jews in Hungary were more assimilated. You know, spoke Hungarian . . ."

The conversation had taken a surreal turn and Rosie wondered if some wine might help. Benyoub had always been a light drinker, and she used to finish his wine. It would almost have been natural to reach for his glass. "I know you didn't come here to talk about my family," Rosie said.

Benyoub smiled awkwardly. "I never met your mother, but I liked your sister."

Rosie knew this was a lie. Did he think it would please her? "My mother died before I came to Paris."

"That's right." He nodded.

She should have encouraged Serge's talk of politics — the National Front was safe. Convenient. Everybody could hate the National Front.

"About the money," she began. "The loan."

"This is very difficult for me . . ." Benyoub interrupted.

"I realize that. Serge and I, we want to help, but we can't give you the full amount. It's not possible. You know Serge has been ill."

Benyoub held his hands together. He looked genuinely uncomfortable, chagrined.

"Right now I'm the only one working. But I can give you, loan you, five thousand francs."

"Did you talk to your friends?" Serge asked. "Will they help?"

"I haven't been able to reach them yet. But I left messages on their answering machines."

Benyoub's friends now had answering machines? Rosie hated talk of money. "I'll give you a check."

"A check?"

Rosie laughed. "I don't keep that kind of money around the house, Ben."

He remained slumped in the chair.

"Most people don't," she added.

"I'll get your purse," Serge offered, standing.

Rosie nodded.

"Can I offer you more wine?" he asked Benyoub, and then noticed his glass, still half full.

"Thank you, no, I don't drink very much."

As Serge left the room Rosie had the sudden impression that Benyoub was looking at her breasts, as if she were an old fertility goddess. Female plenty: milk and money.

"I appreciate this," he said.

"When can you return it?"

"By the end of summer, I hope."

"All right. That's fine. But do you mind if I ask why you need it?"

"Didn't Serge tell you?"

"No. You never told him."

"I thought I had. Are you angry with me?"

The question startled her. "I'm not sure. Perhaps. But I don't mean to be."

"You can't help it," he said. "I didn't behave well."

She was about to agree when Serge entered the room with her purse. "It was a long time ago."

"Not that long," Benyoub replied. "Have you been back to Pittsburgh recently?"

"Pittsburgh, oh God, just say Pittsburgh to me and I think of boiled tongue."

Everyone laughed and she reached for her purse, then took out a checkbook. "Would you turn up the light, Serge? It's getting dark in here." She pulled the cap off a ballpoint pen and smiled at Benyoub. "Are you working now?"

"Off and on. At the same hotel."

She didn't know whether or not to believe him.

"Are you still at Continental?"

He insisted on returning each question as if the evening had been a social one, good friends reflecting over old times. She wrote the check quickly: no point in prolonging his stay. He wouldn't say anything more than he wanted her to know.

"Still there," she assented.

Serge was standing beside her chair. For moral support? She felt glad he hadn't returned to his seat.

"If there's any way I can help you . . ." Benyoub offered.

Rosie looked up at him, puzzled, and then realized he was speaking to Serge.

5

$\mathcal{A}$ WEEK LATER BENYOUB had not yet cashed Rosie's check.

Without mentioning this to Serge, she stopped at her bank to confirm her latest balance, thinking that she needed a new prescription for reading glasses since the print on her balance statement had again begun to blur. Her Thursday afternoon student had canceled, leaving the day free after three o'clock. With Deb arriving on the weekend Rosie decided to use the time to find Benyoub.

It had been years since she'd last seen the Hôtel du Commerce, where Benyoub used to work. The neighborhood's changes startled her. Except for familiar street signs, any vestige of Paris seemed overpowered by North Africa, as if the narrow streets in the Goutte d'Or were determined to have a new identity. Yet this is Paris too, Rosie told herself. As the city absorbed each new group of émigrés, it altered them as well as itself — a kind of double metamorphosis. The nineteenth-century buildings, with their wrought-iron grilles and stucco ornaments, had no loyalties.

A good thing: change triumphing over death. Still, Rosie felt troubled. People against immigration were wrong.

Wrong. The French, an insular people full of self-regard, had to start seeing that. But like everyone else they resisted change. While noble souls like me, Rosie thought, write checks for anyone who comes along with a hand out. She thought of Benyoub again. Only lunatics did such things.

The front door to the hotel was propped open, letting in light from outside as well as the voices of passersby and the honking of car horns. From inside, the opened door seemed to be a rectangle of light to another world, like an image in a surrealist photograph. The walls were tilting almost imperceptibly toward the burning door.

At the reception desk an unfamiliar woman stood shouting into the telephone receiver in a language Rosie assumed to be Arabic. Then the woman caught her eye and turned away, as if she had guessed that the stranger entering the small lobby was not looking for accommodation.

New red wallpaper with an embossed pattern that posed as Imperial made the space darker than Rosie had remembered. A row of plastic plants in need of dusting lined one wall opposite the reception desk, which held several piles of Arabic newspapers, a clipboard with a thick pad of paper, and a brass vase of dried flowers. Above, a wooden ceiling fan slowly revolved.

While waiting for the woman's attention, Rosie reminded herself that she hardly knew Benyoub anymore. Did what she once knew mean anything today?

A long corridor ran from the reception area past the elevator to a small apartment in back of the hotel, where the owner had once lived. The mingling smells of cumin, cleaning fluid, and stale perspiration began to sicken Rosie. Resignation always stank. Beside her stood a wicker table piled with torn magazines.

"Yes?" the woman called. Fortyish, she had stuffed herself into a satiny black dress with a yellow collar. In the soft, flowing clothes of her native country (whatever that was, Rosie thought) she might have appeared handsome. A very faint line of black hairs above her upper lip seemed almost erotic. She had thick, glossy hair.

"I'm looking for someone."

"Yes?" She placed her hands on the counter, as if to push Rosie away.

"He works here. You must know him. Benyoub Benali."

The woman eyed Rosie reluctantly. "Is there some kind of trouble? I don't want any trouble."

"Trouble?" Rosie repeated. "No. I just want to speak with him."

"He hasn't been around for three months. Maybe four. He works for a while, then we don't hear from him until, I suppose, he needs money." She paused, adjusting a loose hairpin at the nape of her neck, and then thought to add, "No one stays very long."

"I saw him last week," Rosie offered.

"Then you've seen him more recently than I have."

Rosie wondered if she were telling the truth. How easily Benyoub had returned to her life, without even trying. "You're infuriating," she wanted to tell him. She could imagine his laughter. He might even have reached out to stroke her hand.

"Would you have an address for him? Or a telephone number?" Rosie asked. "I've misplaced them."

The woman's eyes narrowed, caution becoming suspicion, and Rosie didn't know whether to regret her lie, which must have been transparent, or the abrupt tone of her request.

"It's very important," she added, wishing that she had asked Serge to come along. The woman would have confided in him; people did. In half an hour he would have known all about her beloved grandfather in Tunis, or the failure of her first marriage, or her difficult children — whatever she needed to confess.

Serge had once told Rosie that late at night, when he couldn't sleep, he liked to imagine himself as an invisible time-traveler. Knowing all languages, he joined the courts of the Ptolemys, saw the beheading of queens. And he'd listened to Socrates, Christ, the Buddha. During the day, she thought, he gave the same attention to every encounter. He even carried a small pocket notebook to record memorable remarks. The notebook, he'd said, was part of his examination of the world.

"I have only his address," the woman finally replied. "If you wait a moment I'll write it down."

"That's very kind of you," Rosie said.

The woman stared, as if to ask, "Are you in love with him?" Or, thought Rosie, "You, too?" Her expression was weary, yet imploring. Had she also lent him money? Turning her back on Rosie, she took an address book from a drawer and copied out a line. "I don't think he has a telephone. He doesn't like them."

"I know," Rosie said, immediately hating the air of complicity that was developing. With Ben nothing could be simple.

"You've known him long?" the woman asked.

Rosie hadn't anticipated the question. "More than ten years. Almost fifteen. But we haven't seen each other much recently. Not for years, in fact."

The woman handed her the paper and Rosie saw that the handwriting was exceptionally clear, unlike her own messy scrawl.

"And you?" She didn't want to ask — to know — but it would have seemed rude.

"Only since I've worked here. The last four years."

Rosie stepped back from the counter. "Thank you, really. I appreciate this." The woman's expression held her, and she began to feel uncomfortable.

As Rosie reached the door, the noisy street drew her forward. Then the woman mumbled something. Rosie turned. She couldn't hear exactly, but it sounded like "Don't come back." Yet the woman's face seemed impassive.

Rosie turned away, looking at the address. It was not far from the hotel, within walking distance.

On the sidewalk she took a deep sigh of relief and found herself carried along by a stream of people. Shop windows displayed leather cushions, Arabic books, canned goods with lettering in Arabic script. Several merchants had set up stalls outside their shops, and Rosie recalled the souks in Algiers. She passed bins of umbrellas, flashlights, kitchenware, then piles of blue jeans and rugs rolled up tightly.

Half-veiled women hurried by her, but unlike the Algerian women she remembered, with their eyes cast down, these women looked ahead, their eyes bright. Yet they still made her sad, and even frightened, though she hated admitting this because it seemed the kind of reaction Deb would have, or Aunt Pearl. Before she'd become pregnant with Hamed's child he told her that if she ever carried a child of his she would have to convert to Islam so that they could marry and return to Algeria. The French, he said, never understood important things.

Crossing boulevard Barbès, Rosie smelled the aroma of grilling meat. On the corner a man was selling kebabs of lamb or mutton. Everyone passed him as if he didn't exist. She was tempted but instead reached into her handbag for Benyoub's address. Before she could find it several women surrounded her, and Rosie felt their hands grabbing at her, running over her body, pulling at her handbag. "Get away!" she shouted.

Though the women were so close she could smell their breath, she barely saw them. But she knew they weren't Arabs. In a tight circle, they shoved her back and forth between themselves, making the street spin. "Get away!" she shouted again. A hand tore at her blouse.

Like a stone tossed in water, her struggles seemed to ripple, creating distance between Rosie and everyone else on the street. She had the odd sensation that people were watching, yet the crowd kept moving to its own destination.

"Leave me alone!" she screamed, suddenly aware that the women had taken their hands away and were somehow vanishing into the crowd, as if it welcomed them. The attack had lasted perhaps thirty seconds.

Panting, she staggered across the sidewalk and leaned against the wall of a building. A man walked toward her but she put her hand up instinctively, and he stopped.

She felt her neck with one hand. The thin gold chain was gone. Looking down at her purse, she saw that one of the straps had been cut cleanly — by a knife? She gagged, swallowing her vomit.

Someone touched her shoulder and she jumped.

Beside her stood an elderly Arab woman. "Are you hurt?" she asked.

At first Rosie couldn't reply.

"Are you hurt?"

"No," she said, running her hand through her hair. "I'm all right. Just shaken up."

"Gypsies!" the woman said, spitting out the word.

"Gypsies?"

"Four of them."

Rosie had heard from Polish colleagues that such street attacks were common in Warsaw, but she hadn't known of gypsies in Paris. She tried to catch her breath and looked in her purse.

"You must be careful," the woman said.

"My glasses are gone. They stole my eyeglasses." Rosie started to laugh and the woman drew back.

The man who had almost approached her now went on his way.

"But my wallet's still here," she said, digging deeper into her purse. The idea of being mugged by gypsy women in the middle of a sunny afternoon struck her as absurdly comic. "They only got my eyeglasses and my necklace," she said. "I'm lucky — see? The necklace wasn't worth much."

"You should go home now," the woman said. "I tell my daughters, 'Be careful, the streets aren't safe.'"

Then Rosie noticed that her gold watch was missing from her wrist. "Oh, not that," she sighed. A birthday present from Serge, it had been her favorite piece of jewelry. She held up her wrist. "They got my watch too."

"Do you want a peppermint?" the woman asked.

Why, Rosie wondered, did everything strike her as funny? She shook her head, and then, tasting the residue of vomit in her throat, said, "Please. Yes."

The woman opened her purse, found a small tin of pastilles, and offered them to Rosie.

"Thank you," she said, choosing one. The woman wasn't elderly after all — at most a few years older than Rosie herself.

"Go home now," the woman repeated. She appeared to be satisfied that Rosie could take care of herself.

"Thank you for coming over."

"Remember what I told you. The streets aren't safe any more."

"I'll remember," Rosie said, nodding.

She looked at her empty wrist and sighed again. As long as I'm here, she told herself, hesitating before she opened her purse for Benyoub's address. The paper was gone, but she felt certain that she remembered it correctly.

As she began walking, Rosie was startled by a sharp pain in the hollow of her lower back, where one of the women had punched her. She took several deep breaths before continuing. Around her the street seemed busy — normal — as if nothing had happened. The gypsies were nowhere in sight, but she could still smell the suety kebabs. Her stomach turned. She hated the prospect of telling Serge. He would be kind, he would run her a bath and massage her back, he would know all about gypsies and their virtues.

Walking faster, forcing herself to ignore the pain, Rosie found Benyoub's street. She stopped, rubbed her back below her waist, and then started to look for his building. The search struck her as foolish; she should have just canceled the check.

Recognizing his address, she crossed the street. Like hundreds of other Paris apartment buildings from the turn of the century, this one had a pleasantly seedy facade. Before it stood two middle-aged men, one waving his hands, the other a copy of *El Moudjahid*, an Algerian newspaper. Their argument appeared to be friendly, but Rosie wished they'd picked another place for it. "Excuse me," she said, passing them to step into the courtyard.

She climbed to the third floor and knocked on Benyoub's door. No one answered, but she heard footsteps on the other side.

The hallway was filthy, with paint and plaster chipped from the walls. Rosie guessed that the door at the end of the narrow corridor led to a Turkish toilet. She knocked again, louder.

The door opened slowly, onto a veiled face with questioning eyes.

"I'd like to speak with Benyoub Benali," Rosie said.

The head shook, and Rosie saw that she was speaking to a young girl of fourteen or fifteen.

"I got this address from a friend of his," she said. "At the Hôtel du Commerce."

The girl's eyes narrowed.

"Does Benyoub live here?"

Her head shook again.

"He lives here, doesn't he?"

"No more," she said, slowly closing the door.

"What do you mean? Do you know where I can find him?"

The door shut softly and Rosie knocked again. God*damn* Benyoub! She waited several minutes, then turned back toward the stairs.

6

*Y*OU KNOW, THEY MADE a movie here a couple years ago," Deb said.

"Who?" Rosie asked. "People make movies all over Paris."

"I mean Americans. In this hotel. *Frantic*. Polanski directed it, with Harrison Ford."

"I don't know him."

The sisters stood unpacking Deb's suitcase in her room on the third floor of Le Grand Hôtel. Decorated in a neutral modern style, it struck Rosie as relentlessly bleak. Except for a view of the old rococo opera house, they might have been in Stockholm or Manila.

"Good God, Rosie, you live in Paris, not Timbuktu. He was in . . ."

"I don't go to many American movies."

"Well I don't go all that often either, but I read the newspapers. Did you see that terrycloth bathrobe by the shower? It's mauve!"

"De-luxe," Rosie said.

"We're not going to argue, are we? I didn't come all this way for that."

"Of course not," Rosie said, resisting the urge to add that Deb had only come because she'd won a free trip. "Why don't you have a shower? You must be tired from your flight."

The sisters had tossed their coats on the queen-size bed that dominated the room. Deb wore a short-sleeved, black cotton sweater that fit too tightly, hiking up from the waist of her wrinkled, black cotton skirt. She's always dressed as if she were dissatisfied with civilization, Rosie thought. Deb's hair, a soft brown, had several gray streaks at the temples. Rosie guessed that she needed to lose about forty pounds.

"Here," Deb said, handing Rosie a plastic bag with "FAIRWAY" stamped across the front. "Just a little something."

Rosie opened the bag and burst out laughing at the sight of three packages of Fig Newtons. "Oh I love you. Who else would have remembered? I'm going to have one now."

"And I'll take that shower. Maybe I'm getting too old to fly across oceans."

"You're not even forty yet," Rosie said, tearing open the cellophane.

"All the same," she replied, reaching for her cosmetic case. "We could order some coffee from room service. I'm sure it's ridiculously expensive."

"Do you want to go out, or get some sleep? I could come by later."

"Later? No. I'm up now. Just let me shower. You know, the prize doesn't include room service. Just the room."

Deb disappeared into the bathroom and Rosie listened to the roaring water. Good hotel plumbing, a real Niagara Falls. Deb would probably think it crazy if she asked to try the shower, but at home she'd accustomed herself to a pathetic trickle.

They would not argue. No. They would not spend the time going over old recriminations. If necessary, Rosie would even visit the Louvre again. Anything to keep peace.

Yet since meeting her sister at the airport, Rosie had been waiting for the one unpredictable question that would break her resolve. The first time Deb had come to Paris, almost fifteen years ago, she'd looked at the Turkish toilet down the hall from Rosie's small room and asked, "A communal hole in the floor? How *could* you rent an apartment without a bathroom?" "We don't all use it at once," Rosie had replied, to which Deb answered "Mama's turning over in her grave." Since this was one of the few times Deb had voluntarily mentioned their mother, Rosie felt that she'd hit a bull's-eye. On Deb's next trip, after meeting Benyoub, she'd asked, "How *could* you go with an Arab?" Rosie still liked her reply: "He's not an Arab, his family are Berbers. Like many Algerians." But Deb had shrugged that off with "Aren't you splitting hairs?" Rosie kept wondering what was in store for this visit.

Two sisters who see each other for just one week every few years ought to be able to get along. ("'Ought', 'should', why use such words for feelings?" Serge often asked Rosie.) She couldn't help it, that's what she thought.

"The thing is," Deb said, returning from the shower in the terrycloth robe, an oversized mauve towel wrapped around her head, "people don't understand how much work I put into these trips."

Rosie noticed that Deb's toenails had been painted a bright red, but the color was now chipped, and growing out, so that new half-moons of pink nail abutted the old paint. She wanted to give her a bottle of nail-polish remover at once.

Deb sat on the edge of the bed and began toweling her hair. "I know what people think, but I earn them. Some mornings I have to get up by five-thirty just to address envelopes, if I really want a chance at a prize. I might send in two hundred entries. Add up the postage and envelopes — even if I buy them in bulk — and you'll see the trips aren't free."

Rosie didn't know how to respond.

"And then I might run into a bad spell where I don't win anything for months. It can be a slap in the face. I'm putting out but no return. Just last week I was waiting to hear about a trip to Hawaii: nothing. *Rien.* And I'd really worked hard on that one. I mean it's already July and I've only won three trips this year. A cruise in the Caribbean, tickets to Disney World, and this."

Had Deb finally lost her mind? Rosie wondered, reaching for another Fig Newton. "Who did you take to Disney World?"

"Someone from the office. Recently divorced. I've asked her on several trips already, she travels well. Of course I've won other things this year, don't get me wrong. A ten-speed bicycle, a camcorder, and a man's Rolex. Secondary prizes. But I sold them all."

"How?"

"Through notices on the bulletin board at work. People always like to get new things at half price."

Deb worked for a large educational publisher, editing science textbooks. She was one of the few people Rosie knew who liked her job.

"Why didn't you bring your office friend to Paris?"

"She's seeing a new man," Deb said. "It's at a tricky stage, she couldn't be away for a week."

"Want a Fig Newton?" Rosie asked. She felt she had to say something.

Deb shook her head. "There's still a wife in the picture."

"Ah!"

"You said it."

"Are you sure you don't want to rest? Even a nap?"

"It's almost time for lunch. And maybe we could go to the Louvre. You know I love museums."

Rosie didn't remember that.

"Or we could go shopping. You know me, I'm not like the French, I don't make a fetish of culture."

Rosie forced herself not to respond.

"If you lived in New York I'd take you on some of my trips. Though I'm thinking of giving up contests next year. I want to see how much more I win in this one, but then I'll just enter for things I really want. I know what you're thinking, but it really does take a lot of time. And now that I'm learning Yiddish I have other things on my mind."

"Why Yiddish?" Rosie wished they had ordered some coffee. Her teeth felt coated with the sweet thick paste of figs.

"Everyone's learning it now. I mean, some of the people at my synagogue."

"Why would anyone want to learn Yiddish?"

"Don't they teach it at Continental?"

"We only teach practical languages."

"Sometimes I wish I could talk to Mama now."

"She didn't speak Yiddish."

"How do you know?"

"She never spoke it when we were around. Maybe a word or two of Hungarian. You remember."

"Well she could have."

"I suppose so." This was hardly worth arguing about, Rosie thought.

"She could have," Deb repeated.

The insistent tone of her sister's voice reminded Rosie of their father, although she knew Deb would deny the comparison. She could almost hear Morris saying, "You're supposed to dust the furniture, not scratch it."

"Since when did you start going to synagogue?" Rosie asked.

"I won't discuss it. Not if you use that tone of voice."

"I'm sorry. But Deb, really."

"A couple of years ago I joined a group there. I know you'll laugh. Everyone does. We called it 'Davening for Dates.' But it gives young unmarrieds a chance to meet new people."

As Deb spoke Rosie felt her body had become a heavy weight. The phrase 'young unmarrieds' particularly troubled her.

"I didn't meet anybody I liked but the rabbi, and one thing led to another. Then someone suggested starting a Yiddish group. To learn it, I mean."

"Did you meet anyone there?"

Deb tossed the towel on the floor and propped herself against several fat pillows. "No, but I had the strangest series of messages on my answering machine. It was a man's voice and he'd say 'This is Gerry Gold and I hear you're heaps of fun. I'll try you again,' and sometimes I'd pick up but no one would answer, there was just breathing. And then it stopped."

"Creepy," Rosie agreed. "But living with someone doesn't solve every problem. Serge and I are like an old married couple and I still get lonely and want to make my life better."

"That's different. And I never said I was lonely."

"I just thought . . ."

"Well I didn't. You've always been more practical than me."

Here it comes, Rosie thought. Brace yourself. Ask her something first — anything. "Were you entering contests the last time I saw you, at Daddy's funeral?"

"It doesn't seem possible that was only three years ago. I'd already started. Just a few. In fact I had on the Longines watch I'd just won. It was too dressy for work."

Rosie put the package of Fig Newtons on the blond-wood bureau, annoyed that she'd eaten a third of it.

"Around then," Deb said, "I decided that if I couldn't find a husband at least I'd see the world. And publishing salaries stink."

"No one gets rich at Continental either."

"They're all pigfuckers. You give and you give and you give, and you get slapped in the face."

"But you like your Yiddish?" Rosie asked, reeling from the violence in her sister's words.

"It'll be several years before I can read comfortably."

"Is there anybody writing in Yiddish you'd want to read?" Rosie kept feeding Deb questions, and began to feel that there was something nasty in doing it. But it was a way of not talking about herself.

"Isaac Bashevis Singer, for God's sake! He only won a Nobel Prize. And he lives not far from me, at 85th and Broadway. His building's a shrine. When I pass it at night sometimes I look up and wonder which window is his. He's supposed to have windows on Broadway."

"I've never read anything of his."

"I know where Singer eats lunch — he's vegetarian. One time I followed him into the restaurant . . ."

"You were following him?"

"I saw him walking on 73rd Street and all of a sudden I guessed that he was going into Eclair's, so when he did I went in too. While I was waiting for my schnitzel he was eating some kind of soup, and I wanted to go over and say something, because I know he wouldn't have minded, but I couldn't think what to say. So I lost my chance."

"He would probably have told you to enjoy your lunch."

Deb laughed. "I thought that, later. It's probably just as well I didn't say anything." She continued laughing, apparently pleased with the notion of Singer wishing her a good meal.

"I have an idea," Rosie said. "Instead of going out to lunch, let's visit Serge. We'll eat at my place. You want to see Serge again, don't you?"

"Whatever you say," Deb said. "I'm all yours."

Rosie didn't like the sound of that but took a quick mental survey of the contents of her refrigerator. She could make omelettes, and there was some leftover ratatouille. By now Serge would have picked up a baguette. "Then we'll go back to my place. There's all week to see the Louvre."

"I'd better put on some clothes," Deb yawned, without moving.

Serge would help, Rosie thought. He'll take off some of the pressure. Maybe he would show Deb the canal walk — he'd understand. Seven more days. And Deb hadn't yet asked her the question, whatever it might be.

Fifteen minutes later, in front of the hotel, Rosie was about to direct Deb to the left, toward the Métro, when a magazine-pretty doorman asked, *"Taxi, Madame?"*

She nodded and instantly found herself pushing Deb into a taxi. It was wasteful, an unnecessary luxury, but the prospect of leading her sister across the city by subway immobilized Rosie. She only hoped that Deb wouldn't expect to make a habit of it.

As their driver sped through the streets, Deb slumped down in the seat, resting her head comfortably against it. "Maybe I should have napped a bit," she offered. "I am exhausted."

"You can rest at my place." Rosie looked out the window as they passed a block of unfamiliar buildings. Since she rarely used taxis, and knew few people who owned cars, the trip seemed like an event, the start of a holiday, or of a funeral. The last time she'd sat beside Deb like this had been in the limousine at their father's funeral: Rosie tried to side-step the memory. Somewhere Deb had gotten hold of a book about modern Jewish etiquette and insisted they follow its advice — "I hope this won't make you angry," she'd said. Then she'd stood in Morris's kitchen reading passages aloud until Rosie gave in and let her run the day. Fortunately Serge had remained back in Paris. He hated shows of piety — medievalism, he called them. Holy books were only books of etiquette.

"Have you been back to Daddy's grave?" Rosie asked, regretting the question immediately.

Deb opened her eyes and stared at Rosie. "I hope I never set foot in Pittsburgh again."

"Oh."

Let her rest, nap, sleep. Maybe exhaustion was catching. Rosie wanted to crawl into bed and bury her face in her pillow. She would sleep for five years.

As they climbed out of the taxi and Rosie tipped the African driver, Deb looked about. "I don't know why people say New York is dirty. It doesn't hold a candle to Paris."

"You think this is dirty?"

"I mean Needle Park is practically my front yard, but . . ."

"The homeless are everywhere," Rosie said, wishing that the remark hadn't sounded so dismissively cosmopolitan. She led the way into her building, turning on the light for the stairwell.

"I've never understood these French hallways," Deb said. "Why can't they leave the lights on all the time?"

"It's a waste of electricity." Rosie clenched her teeth.

"It can't cost that much extra. With everybody turning them off and on all the time . . ."

"They've done studies," Rosie said. And maybe they had.

As Rosie turned her key in the door, Serge pulled it open. "Ah Deborah! Deborah!" He took Deb's hands in his, then kissed her cheeks. "*Ça va?* Did you have a good flight?"

Bless Serge, thought Rosie. Though he was putting it on a bit thick.

"We're having lunch here," Rosie said to him. "You'll join us?"

"But of course."

Who was he imitating? Maurice Chevalier? Deb didn't seem to notice.

"Would anyone else like a Lillet?" Rosie asked, heading to the kitchen.

"A drink would put me to sleep," Deb said, tossing herself on the sofa.

"Have you been cooking?" Rosie asked. "What do I smell?"

"Benyoub brought that by. An hour ago. You just missed him."

Rosie didn't know which way to turn. "Benyoub? What do you mean?"

"It's a vegetable couscous. He said it would make me healthy." Serge's face revealed nothing.

"Two days ago I couldn't even find where he lived."

"Wasn't Benyoub your Arab?" Deb asked.

"Yes," Rosie said. "My Arab.

7

$\mathcal{I}$N THE FOLLOWING DAYS Rosie did her best
to avoid thinking of Benyoub, but with little success. Since
she had no way of reaching him, Deb's visit became a welcome distraction. By the time she next went to the bank, her
check to Benyoub had been cashed. She supposed he would
vanish now, until the end of summer. Yet his curious gift
continued to trouble her. So personal, it seemed a violation.

She even dreaded tasting the food. Had he actually
made it, or simply gone into a restaurant and ordered a
take-out serving? The bowl had a thin crack along its edge
— a nice, homey detail. And the couscous tasted familiar:
his recipe. Somewhere he must have a kitchen, or access to
one. Perhaps the hotel woman, or the young veiled girl, had
warned him of her pursuit. The couscous was a gesture to
throw her off guard. She resented it, though Serge insisted
that Benyoub had appeared sincere in his concern for his
health. It might even be possible. After all, thought Rosie,
Serge was not easily charmed. But she didn't want Benyoub
in her thoughts.

Deb had suggested that they visit the Jewish quarter of
Paris, to seek out old synagogues. "We could go to Père

Lachaise and look up Sarah Bernhardt," Rosie had offered. Anything to keep Benyoub at bay. Deb, however, was wedded to synagogues.

"What *is* this about?" Rosie wanted to know.

"I don't like that question," Deb had replied.

Then Rosie remembered Morris during her annual summer visits home. "I don't like that question," he'd often answer to inquiries about his health. After he'd retired and sold the house, he moved into a small senior-citizen's apartment on the edge of a shopping mall and, apparently, prepared to die. It took ten years of waiting, of hot lunches for a dollar and afternoon bingo at the Jewish Community Center, of organized bus trips to Amish country, or the zoo, where he sat at a table with other golden-agers, watching busloads of disadvantaged children, also on organized day trips, terrorizing each other. Rosie had even joined several excursions, winning sympathy as a good daughter from the aging women who still, as one said, liked "having a fella." Morris became a celebrity of sorts: his daughter from Paris visited every summer.

When he died, Rosie had remained in Pittsburgh for a week to empty his apartment. One morning she found a cardboard box of her old textbooks in the back of the hall closet. Leafing through them she put several aside to take back to Paris. *Bleak House, The Book of the Hopi.* At the bottom of the box was a used copy of Freud's *Future of an Illusion,* which she read again, that night, in the nearly empty living room, curled up in her father's battered recliner. Religion was an illusion, and no sane person held to illusions. A lost cause, a dead end, and poor compensation for human suffering. "I know how difficult it is to avoid illusions," Freud had written. From her chair Rosie had looked out on the darkening night sky — the drapes already given to Mrs. Dworkin, two floors up — and tried to recall

Morris's face. "In the long run nothing can withstand reason and experience, and the contradiction religion offers to both is too palpable."

The book must be somewhere in her apartment, along with a guide to Père Lachaise she'd bought years ago. Maybe she would give them to her sister. But what did Deb think she'd found? Certainly not God. For nowhere was it written that God loved stockings with runs, food-stained skirts, contest entries, davening for dates. And not-so-young unmarrieds. Wherever an overweight fortyish woman sat alone, ringless, her despair palpable (a nice word, Rosie thought) sat proof that God had looked away. Who in their right mind would ask him for comfort?

But Deb refused all discussions of religion until Rosie feared it had been a mistake to take a week of her holidays while she was in Paris. Instead Deb complained constantly of being tired, and in spite of their museum plans, she and Rosie sat around talking. Rosie knew that they were both trying to keep to safe subjects, but an hour with her became a minefield. She disliked the way Deb made her feel that she had to justify living in Paris. At a certain point you either stayed for good or you went back home she'd always told friends, certain that her point had long passed. "Just because I was born in America shouldn't mean I have to waste my time with its particular hangups," she remarked. If religion was off limits, she would also close the door on further discussions of America's superiority to Europe. Fortunately Deb had a hotel room.

One morning, as Rosie entered the lobby of Le Grand Hôtel, she felt grateful that she'd just visited a new dermatologist, a Danish woman who told her to wash her hair like a cashmere sweater. Deb would certainly like that detail. Rosie wouldn't add that the doctor thought her problem might come from nerves, and had also referred her to a gynecologist, but she was ready to describe her weekly regime of vitamin shots, or discuss the virtues of the herbal tea she was supposed to drink while giving up coffee.

Spotting her, Deb hurried over, exclaiming, "The pigfuckers! Pigfuckers!"

"What happened?" Rosie asked, noting that her sister didn't appear to be hurt. "What's going on?"

A man behind the reception desk, in an expensive dark suit and tie, stood watching them, Rosie thought, with a patronizing air. Who did he think he was? The arrogant bastard.

"This has never happened before. And I've been all over the world. I've been to . . ."

"Calm down," Rosie interrupted. Something had agitated Deb until her face had turned red. "Calm down and tell me what happened."

"'What happened?' What do you think happened? Some goddam Frenchie pigfucker stole my wallet. That's what happened."

"Where?" Rosie sighed.

"I told you that Needle Park is practically in my front yard, but I had to come all the way to Paris to get robbed."

"The streets aren't safe," Rosie said.

"I wasn't on the street. It was right here, in the hotel. I had my wallet in my room, I checked because I took some francs from my money belt and put them in my wallet before coming down to meet you — it's a damn good thing I wear a money belt or I'd be in big trouble — and I was going to cash another traveler's check so I went to the counter and opened my purse and saw I'd been robbed."

"Did you check in your room . . ."

"That's what the hotel clerk said. So helpful. I told him to go look if he wanted, but I knew my wallet had been stolen. There was a crowd registering for some fashion convention and someone brushed against me; that's when it must have happened. The police think so too."

Deb seemed so caught up in telling the story that Rosie didn't have the heart to interrupt again.

"Of course the goddam manager wants to keep things hush-hush, but I told him a thing or two. The pigfucker got all my credit cards, my social security card, the membership card for my video club . . ."

"What did the police say?"

". . . my library card, it's a good thing I don't drive or they'd have my driver's license too. You know how police are, I had to fill in some reports, but they doubt anyone will use the cards, hotel thieves are usually too scared of being caught, they're just after money. And they didn't get much of that. Maybe eighty bucks in francs. But I had to work for it. Every penny. Some contests give a thousand dollars spending money with a trip, but not this one."

"What should we do now?"

"I've already reported the stolen credit cards — you're half an hour late, you know — so I guess I can go out and enjoy Paris. I'm not going to let this spoil my holiday."

"My doctor was running late."

"Doctors, don't give me doctors. We'll have some lunch and then take in a museum. Is there a McDonald's around here?"

"I know a bistro nearby that makes the best pâté sandwiches, with cornichons. It's not far from my office."

"All right. Whatever. Though McDonald's is fine with me."

After crossing the Place de l'Opéra Rosie led them down a small cobblestone side street barely wider than an alley. "Some friends of Serge asked us to dinner tonight, to welcome him home from the hospital. They said to invite you."

"I don't usually go out at night when I travel. It's better to save energy for sight-seeing."

"Well we haven't been doing much of that. And I thought you might like to see a French home."

"I'll come. Sure. But do you think a party's a good idea for Serge? You know liver problems can be serious."

"Don't say that."

"But it's true."

"What did he tell you?"

"Just that he was having a little liver trouble. But I knew better. He drinks too much, doesn't he?"

There it was! Rosie thought: the question. Sneaking up on her, waiting for the right moment, then pouncing. Just the way it always did. "No," Rosie replied. "He doesn't drink too much."

"Well I only mentioned it to be polite. Don't get offended. With all the science books I've edited, I've learned a thing or two about the human body."

Rosie suddenly decided she didn't want to take Deb into her favorite bistro, though her sister was already eyeing a *tarte aux pommes* in the window. If someone from the school was there, and Deb started to recount her morning's adventure, it would be humiliating. "Your idea was better. If we keep walking we'll get to a McDonald's soon."

"But this place looks nice," Deb said tentatively.

"Oh, when the *tarte aux pommes* hits the window," Rosie said, wondering where to take her lie, "well, it's usually a couple of days old by then." Rosie kept walking, decisively, and Deb hurried along to catch up. "You really should see a French dinner party, and who knows when you'll win another trip to Paris?"

By the time Deb went back to her hotel for a nap, Rosie was anxious to see Serge. The almost-discussion of his liver had haunted her through the afternoon. Deb really might have learned things from the books she edited. Sinister, medical facts.

Serge was in the bathroom, his chin and cheeks covered with shaving cream. "A nice day?" he called as she kicked off her shoes.

"Okay," she called back. "I think she's had her fill of the Louvre."

"You missed Benyoub again."

Rosie grimaced. "What do you mean?"

"He telephoned twice. The first time just after you left, around nine, and then an hour ago, around four."

"What did he want?"

"I don't know. To talk. I told him we enjoyed the couscous."

"That's all?"

"Really, Rosie, he was almost sweet. He wanted to know how I was feeling . . ."

"What did you tell him?"

"That I'm better."

She crossed their bedroom and leaned against the door frame while he continued to shave. "Are you?" she asked.

"Of course I am. You can see."

"I worry about you."

"Well don't. What happened at the dermatologist's?"

Rosie described the vitamin shots and herbal tea. "She asked if I'm a controlling person. Do you think I am?"

"You worry too much."

"That's not an answer."

"Then I don't know what she means."

"Come on, Serge. Am I controlling? I don't think so."

"Never listen to doctors."

"You know what else she told me? She said that I had nursing breasts."

"Good God! What were you discussing? I like your breasts though." He winked at her in the mirror. "Always have."

Rosie thought that the harsh bathroom light seemed to make his shoulder blades stick out even more sharply than usual. Poor Serge. What a sad, forlorn thing, the body. She looked away from him. The purple wallpaper she'd chosen to match dark purple towels had been a mistake. Stepping into the small space, she put her arms around Serge. "I'm glad," she said softly.

He scraped the last spot of lather from his neck and held his razor blade under the running hot water. "I have an idea," he said.

Such pale skin, Rosie thought, rubbing her cheek against his shoulder. "What is it?" While black hair covered his chest, in the center was a diamond-shaped gray patch.

"Remember sometimes we used to . . ."

"I remember."

He turned, kissing her gently, and with one hand she undid the zipper of her skirt. It fell to the floor while Serge helped pull her jersey blouse over her head. Tossing the rest of their clothes aside, they clung to each other for a moment and then Serge sat on the toilet, drawing Rosie toward him. She straddled his lap and he leaned his face against her breasts. "Wet me," he whispered.

Bending, she caressed his back, closing her arms around him as his mouth searched for a nipple. "Wet me," he repeated.

She found herself looking at a box of Arpege bath powder on the toilet tank, which seemed to become clearer, more detailed, with each touch of his fingers around her waist. Their bodies breathed together until she felt her urine flow. Serge pressed against her, hard, and she whispered, "I love you."

Soon she lifted herself up, mounting his erection, and began to move slowly. Her nipples tingled as his arms pulled her close, but almost at once she felt a shudder run through his body. She knew he was finished, that any second he would be ready to let go of her, leave her body to itself. She wanted to cry.

"I'd better wash," he finally said.

"Don't move yet," she replied, staring at her arms around his back.

"I love you, Rosie."

"Yes, I know."

He laughed softly.

"What is it?"

"Nursing breasts!"

She clasped her arms tighter. "Who are you?" she asked. "Tell me."

"I'm your husband . . . your father . . . your son . . . your brother . . . your lover."

"And I'm your wife . . . your mother . . . your sister . . . your daughter . . ."

"Will you hand me a towel?"

Rosie kissed his right ear. "If I asked, would you cut off your ear like van Gogh did, and send it to me?"

"I'll have to think about that."

She pulled back and he steadied her with his hands as she stood before him. "Then get your own towel," she said, softly.

When they let go of each other she felt a spasm of pain run through her body. It didn't seem possible that she would be able to stand alone. "I wish we weren't going out," she said.

"Is your sister coming?"

Rosie nodded and began running a bath. "Thierry doesn't know what they're getting into."

"She's a sad girl, Rosie."

"Don't call her a girl. Please." There was never any point in talking about Deb, Rosie thought. "Did Benyoub leave a number?"

"He said he'd call back."

By the time they arrived at the Roussels' apartment building on Avenue Kléber, Rosie had accustomed herself to the idea of a rocky evening.

"You said they're Communists?" Deb asked.

"Yes," Rosie hesitated.

"Then what are they doing in a place like this?"

"Thierry inherited it earlier this year from an aunt." The old stone building seemed to exhale money and ease.

"Nice work," Deb said. She wore a well-cut, black cotton dress that Rosie thought flattering.

While taking the lift to the Roussels' floor, Deb admired the bronze grillwork that had been polished to a golden sheen. "Do they have a big apartment?" she asked.

"Wait and see," Rosie said. "But I should warn you about one thing. Renée collects antique needlework, and if you show any interest it all comes out."

"But I would be interested," Deb said.

The elevator door opened and Rosie saw two unfamiliar men talking with the Roussels outside the door to their apartment. Serge walked ahead more quickly.

"It's not a question of punishment," Renée was saying, in a voice higher than usual. Then Thierry put his arm around her. Rosie could tell that she'd just splashed on some Cabochard, a scent she might have worn if it wouldn't have seemed like an imitation of Renée's good taste. But something must have interrupted her at the dressing table — she wore no lipstick. The sight of her friend's naked lips startled Rosie. It was a matter of pride with Renée that she could eat an entire meal and keep her lipstick on; she had been raised that way.

"Look what they did, Serge!" Renée reached to embrace him.

As Rosie came closer she saw a crudely carved swastika on the gleaming black door.

"We should never have moved in here," Thierry said to Rosie.

"Are you blaming me?" Renée asked.

"But you're not Jewish," Rosie said.

"Some of the people in this building are so right-wing," Thierry replied, staring at the swastika, "I don't even like to think about it."

"But why you?" Rosie insisted.

"Does it matter?" Thierry put one finger on the gashed door, where the swastika cut into the wood.

"I just don't understand."

"When a few neighbors started praising Le Pen I had some words to say. And it's probably gotten around that we're in the Party. You never know."

"Of course we can't prove a thing," Renée added.

"Europe!" murmured Deb.

Startled, Rosie felt almost certain that no one had heard her. She wondered if Deb could have followed much of the exchange, which took place in French. Perhaps she recognized Le Pen's name. Rosie regretted that the Roussels spoke English — the evening might be safer if Deb couldn't understand a word.

Without introducing the two men, who now watched quietly, Thierry suggested that Rosie take Deb into the apartment.

High ceilings with ornate plaster flowers in the center, and large French windows overlooking the street, dwarfed the few pieces of furniture in the living room. The sofa and chairs had been artfully draped with heavy white sheets, and for a moment Deb looked puzzled, as if she'd mistakenly entered the closed-up house of a family away on vacation. There were no rugs on the dark wood floors, and their footsteps echoed. All color had been blotted up from the room.

"I know what you're thinking," Rosie said.

"It's beautiful," Deb replied. "But sort of creepy too."

The apartment smelled sweetly of tarragon, and Rosie knew that Renée had made her standard roast chicken. It was the only dish she served guests, although the accompanying vegetables might vary. Renée and Thierry soon joined them, with Serge. "I'm sorry, we should have introduced you," Thierry apologized. "They were neighbors, from the tenants' association. We'd just discovered the swastika and telephoned them."

Still visibly shaken, Renée asked if anyone would like an aperitif.

"Nothing red for me," Deb said. "I never drink red wine. The tannin kills me. What are my options?"

"We have vodka," Thierry suggested.

"Vodka, yes. And tonic. Please. With lots of ice. I read in some magazine that the French never use ice. Why is that?"

"I use ice," Thierry said.

Rosie and Serge asked for wine, and Thierry left the room.

"I love your collection," Deb said, standing before a large framed piece of white-on-white embroidery, about three feet square. "Where's this from?"

"It's Macedonian," Renée said, without her customary enthusiasm. "I bought it at a flea market in Belgrade."

"Is it old?"

"Very. And it's museum quality. The woman selling it said it had been in her family for years. Probably part of a bridal outfit, the work's so fine."

"I wouldn't mind having it," Deb said admiringly.

Rosie sank into her chair, as if she were a spectator. She knew that she was about to fail everyone, but tonight she lacked the will to censor Deb. And she was surprised that Renée hadn't taken her sister by the arm for the grand tour, but left Deb standing by herself.

Thierry returned with a black lacquer tray of drinks and

said, "I must apologize again for the commotion. We were so shocked . . ."

"There's nothing to apologize for," Serge interrupted, taking his glass. "I would have been shocked too."

"Why are you all so surprised?" Deb asked.

Everyone turned to her.

"I mean, in Europe that's how they treat Jews, isn't it?"

"Deb!" Rosie said, cringing.

"Well the French have nothing to be proud of. They were horrible."

"Not all French people supported the Nazis," Renée said, agitated. "In fact I've personally always regretted not being Jewish."

"More did than like to admit it," Deb continued. "And from what I just saw on your door, I'd say the impulse is alive and well. It's nice to pretend the past didn't happen, but my mother was in one of the camps. We're children of a survivor; we can't afford to pretend."

"You never mentioned that," Thierry said, looking at Rosie with a new interest.

"I don't talk about it," she replied.

"In Hungary, that's where my mother was interned first," Deb said.

Please, oh please, Rosie thought, don't call them all pig-fuckers.

"But what Rosie said is true. Children of survivors often don't talk about it. They feel ashamed. Isn't that awful? I'm part of a research study at Columbia about children of survivors."

"You never told me," Rosie said.

"We're not supposed to talk about it outside our group. You get started talking and out come memories, and then you forget who you've told. Oral history isn't just a matter of people talking. It takes work."

"But that has nothing to do with Europe," Renée said.

"Sure it does. And that's how I know so much about the French. Let me tell you, they've got plenty to answer for. It makes coming to Europe very difficult for me."

"Then why do you come?" Renée asked.

Rosie slumped in her chair.

"Well I've got a sister here, you know that. And I'm not afraid of the past. I want to confront it. That's a very American trait."

"But in the United States," Renée said, "the blacks have suffered horribly. Europe didn't invent racism."

"Who do you think brought the slaves to America? Europeans, that's who. And no matter what anyone says, American blacks have the highest standard of living in the world. And there were no death camps."

"I don't think it's that simple," Thierry said. "Perhaps we should change the subject."

"I'm not afraid of it if you aren't," Deb replied. "You know what they say, 'if you don't remember the past you're condemned to repeat it.'" She took several sips of her drink as the telephone rang.

"I'd better get that," Renée excused herself. "It might be about the door."

"Why don't you sit down?" Rosie said, indicating a space for Deb on the sofa beside her. Suddenly the sheet-covered furniture struck her as an unpleasant affectation, though Renée had probably intended it to be clever.

"Yes, I will. And if you hand me my purse, I've brought something to show everyone."

Deb reached into her large handbag and took out a thick stack of photographs. "These are pictures from my last trip. A cruise in the Caribbean. I thought you might enjoy seeing them. We spent two nights in Martinique, it's very French, you know."

"I didn't think you'd brought the pictures," Rosie said.

"You liked them so much I thought everyone should have the chance to see them." Then she smiled at Thierry. "You've invited me into your home like this, the least I can do is share my pictures with you."

Serge held up his empty glass for a refill and Rosie saw Thierry wink.

"But we shouldn't start until Renée comes back," Deb said. "She'll want to see them too."

Rosie looked at her inexpensive new watch. At least two hours before they could leave.

8

"YOU COULD SAY I'M LUCKY," Deb suggested, handing Rosie her stolen wallet, which the police had brought to the hotel the night before.

"I wish there was time for me to buy you a new one," Rosie said.

They sat lingering in Deb's hotel room on Sunday morning, her packed suitcases waiting by the door. Rosie examined the red leather wallet. It was streaked with water marks.

"The police found it in Place Vendôme," Deb said. "At least my credit cards are all here."

"You were right, they only wanted money."

"I guess so."

"But it smells awful," Rosie said.

"It must have been out in that rain on Thursday."

"Why don't you throw it out now?" Rosie asked.

"I should." Deb took the wallet and began removing her credit cards.

"If it rains heavily for days," Rosie said, "my kitchen gets so damp — the old walls are rotting — that sometimes little mushrooms push out through the wallpaper behind the sink."

Deb shuddered. "Don't you miss the States? That would never happen at home."

"It's funny, but the last time I was back I didn't like all that depressing grass everywhere — just too much green. I missed the old stone here. Are you sure you don't want me to come to the airport?"

"No, it's a boring ride. We can say goodbye downstairs."

"It seems like you just came."

"Doesn't it?" Deb tossed the empty wallet into a wastebasket beside her chair. Making a pile of the credit cards, she leaned back in a slouch.

Rosie was surprised that she felt upset about Deb's departure. "Maybe I'll visit you next summer."

"It's too bad you don't live in New York. Then you could come with me on my trips. I don't always like traveling with Helen — she talks too much. Sometimes it drives me crazy."

"I thought she was your best friend."

"She is. But you know me. I'm always criticizing people."

"Oh, Deb."

"It's like something's wrong with me, so I criticize people and then feel bad about it. I might as well go off and stick pins in myself."

"Don't say that."

"No. It's true. But it's a common trait in children of survivors. We feel guilty about everything. And we're very critical."

"I'm like that too," Rosie confessed. If that was how Deb saw herself, then it might be a family habit. "Just ask Serge. Always seeing slights and snubs . . ."

"At least you've got Serge. But he doesn't look well."

Rosie stiffened. She wouldn't let herself be irritated by Deb now. "I don't know why you say that."

"Make him eat properly. Nutrition's important."

"Next week we're going to his mother's, in the country. It'll do him good to get out of Paris."

"Bring him to New York next summer, if you come."

"He might have trouble getting in. You know, being a Communist."

"Life would be easier in the States," Deb said. "You don't even have a video player."

"My appreciation of technology stopped with the stereo."

"Suit yourself," Deb laughed. "But a video player's a nice thing."

"I hate American materialism."

"And the French aren't materialistic?"

"You know I hate being forty." Rosie sighed. "Everything goes by so fast."

"We'd better get down to the lobby," Deb said, rising from her chair. "It's almost time for my limo."

Rosie watched her stuff the loose credit cards into a compartment in her purse and then wander through the hotel room, checking that she hadn't left anything behind. This grim, matronly frump, her sister, seemed trapped by the furniture. "I wish you weren't going already," Rosie said. Probably Deb wouldn't believe her.

"Whenever there's a contest for Paris, I enter it," Deb replied. "What are you doing this week?"

"I need new reading glasses. And I'm meeting Benyoub this afternoon. Here, let me help with the suitcases."

"I'm balanced," Deb said, but Rosie insisted on taking the larger one from her. "Not your Arab?"

"You liked his couscous," Rosie said.

Deb smiled. "I hope you know what you're doing."

"We're still friends. Sort of. It would be a shame to live with someone for five years and then not be able to speak with them."

"I wouldn't know. To me it's *meshuga*." She picked up her room key from the bureau. "We're off. Goodbye Paris!"

When Deb's limousine drove away from the hotel Rosie stood feeling as if she had failed someone again, in an obscure way that she might never understand. Deb must have been exaggerating about her griefs. People always did, their troubles, problems, neuroses becoming possessions like heirloom silver, polished in the telling. For a moment Rosie almost envied Deb her contests, her Yiddish lessons, the survivor group at Columbia. Deb would be fine. What choice did she have?

In the Place Vendôme, not far from the hotel, several busloads of Japanese with cameras were photographing the graceful obelisk. Quickening her step, Rosie headed for the Seine, where she often liked to walk. But she noticed nothing, took nothing in. She might as well have been back in Pittsburgh for all that she saw around her: poor Deb, poor dead Morris, poor dead Aunt Pearl (cancer of the throat), Uncle Aladar locked up in a nursing home, in an Alzheimer fog, the dreary cousins married and breeding, with obscenely large expanses of neat suburban lawns surrounding their relentlessly happy full lives.

Rosie walked faster.

Poor dead Mama and her pills.

Faster, faster.

The old childhood house, who lived in it now? Soon, she thought, there would be no one left who remembered her as a child, no one who stood between her and death.

A critic, a complainer: so that was how Deb saw herself. Family habit? Rosie wondered. Self-pity was a horrible emotion, and some people didn't seem to have very much of it — or they never showed it. But she wasn't sure they experienced it either.

Finally reaching the river, Rosie leaned against the stone embankment and looked into the brownish green water. Serge had promised to spend the day reading Renée's manuscript, so she had no reason to go back to the apartment. Sunday in Paris meant you had to belong. Except for Serge, if she never saw the apartment again she wouldn't mind. How arbitrary it seemed that she had saved certain books to read again or carefully looked after the Moroccan bowls. If only she'd mentioned that to Deb. Did she find much of her life arbitrary too?

Yesterday Deb had surprised Rosie, saying, "Last night I couldn't fall asleep and started wondering what happened to our old dolls." Rosie had no idea, but described the books she'd found in Morris's closet: "I even brought a few back to Paris, but I've never looked at them." "Daddy couldn't throw out books," Deb had offered. "The last time I saw him, he showed me a box of mine. There was a paperback of *Marjorie Morningstar* so I took it with me. It held up pretty well." "I loved that!" Rosie had exclaimed. At fourteen, she had longed to be grownup like Marjorie. Grownup, far from Pittsburgh.

A critic, a complainer. Runs in the family, where misery loves company.

Rosie wished that she had insisted on going to the airport with Deb instead of agreeing to meet Benyoub. When he'd called early that morning, hoping to see her in the afternoon, even Serge had thought it was a good idea. But now it seemed pointless. Perhaps he'd changed his mind too.

Retracing her steps, Rosie arrived fifteen minutes early at the Place de la Madeleine. Its grand church was undergoing renovations and had been surrounded by a large tarpaulin that made her think of a massive bandage. Benyoub already stood waiting, and greeted Rosie with a kiss on each check. Again he wore a freshly laundered white shirt, which flattered his dusky skin.

"I've been trying to find you," he said.

"Why didn't you leave a phone number? I'm not that hard to reach."

"I never know where I'll be next." He took her by the arm and headed toward a restaurant with tables set up on the sidewalk. "We can sit here. Is this all right?"

"It's fine. Yes."

They selected the table farthest from the door and Benyoub pulled out a chair for Rosie. Five thousand francs, she thought, at least bought good manners. She wondered if he had enough money for an espresso. In the past she usually paid. Surely he wasn't on a student visa any more.

"Do you want something to eat?" asked Benyoub.

She shook her head. "Just coffee."

He picked up a paper napkin and folded it in half, then in quarters.

"I went to the hotel. Did the receptionist tell you?" She thought his eyes darkened. Nearby several cars began honking their horns, but she didn't bother to look.

"No."

He was probably bedding the woman. "And she gave me an address, where a young girl pretended not to know you."

"I don't like people following me." He unfolded the napkin and smoothed it flat.

"I was hardly doing that. I'd given you a check, for a large amount of money, and after a week you still hadn't cashed it. Since the money had seemed so urgent I wanted to know what was going on."

"You could have canceled it."

"Maybe I should have. But I'd given my word."

"I was away for a few days."

"Away?"

"In Marseilles."

"A vacation?"

"No."

Marseilles, she knew, was a center of the National Front. "Are you involved in some political thing? Some kind of protest or . . ."

"I don't want to talk about it. Let's just say I was on vacation."

"But you're up to something," she said, and then decided not to press the issue. He was probably working against the mullahs who wanted to run Algeria. Yes, that would be like Ben.

"Believe what you want, but I don't have to go into my affairs with anyone."

Meeting him had been a mistake.

"You have all the luck," he said, running his thumb along the creased edge of the napkin.

"What do you mean?"

"A nice place to live, someone to take care of you."

"Life isn't that simple. You know better."

"Then what am I supposed to think about you?"

"Say I'm dead. Whatever you like."

"Rosie! Don't talk like that."

"Then think of me as a married woman."

An elderly woman passed their table with a small, scruffy dog. Her cane kept bumping against its hind leg, but the animal didn't appear to notice. The air smelled of gasoline.

"Are you and Serge married? He didn't say . . ."

"I don't have to go into my affairs with anyone."

In spite of themselves, they laughed.

Suddenly she thought of Hamed. "How is your cousin?"

"Praying five times a day," Benyoub said impatiently.

It seemed inevitable. Ben and Hamed had never gotten along; "bad blood" was all Ben used to offer as explanation. But Rosie knew that no one could nurse a grudge better than

Benyoub — except for herself. Hadn't Serge often reminded her that grudges were pointless?

Benyoub leaned forward, against the table. "There's still something between us."

"You'd like to think that, wouldn't you? Men always want to believe they're the only one."

"But it's true. Isn't it?"

"The idea's tiresome, Ben. It's been years since we mattered to each other."

"I think you're lying."

"I'll tell you something that's true. I resent the way you've been using Serge to get to me."

"He's a kind man, I haven't been using him. We've had some interesting talks. His politics are very solid."

"Oh great."

"That matters to me."

"Why is it that I don't believe you?"

"Rosie, Rosie, it's terrible the way you talk. You've become cynical."

"Why did you ask to see me?"

"After the other night I was worried about you. I wonder if you appreciate Serge."

"What a rotten thing to say. I didn't have to come here, you know."

"You wanted to come here."

Deb had been right, the meeting was a mistake. "If you got money from your friends in Marseilles, you can repay the loan."

"But we agreed on the end of summer. I don't have it now."

"Okay, Ben, you win."

"I don't think you appreciate Serge. You want to know why?"

"No. I don't."

Benyoub looked about for a waiter.

"And don't try to tell me," Rosie added. "Leave Serge out of this."

"There's something I want to ask you."

Rosie watched him.

"When I came to your apartment, and Serge was there, why did you say you hadn't liked Algeria?"

"I never said that."

"Did you think he would find it disloyal? You remember how I borrowed my cousin's car so that we could drive south, because you wanted to see the desert."

"Yes."

"And you said that you'd never seen anything as peaceful, or as frightening."

"The desert was beautiful."

"Well?"

"Well what? I haven't thought of it since then."

"People don't forget the desert."

"Maybe once or twice," she corrected herself. If they were to end the meeting amicably she would have to indulge him.

"Do you really want coffee?"

"No," she replied.

"Why don't we walk instead?"

A new black Renault turned the corner of rue Tronchet and pulled up beside the curb, several feet from the table, parking illegally. As Rosie moved to push back her chair, a handsome, unveiled Arab woman in her early thirties got out of the car with a small boy of five or six who reached for her hand. She ignored his gesture and headed to the rear of the car, the boy now following her. Before Rosie could tell what was happening, the boy dropped his pants and squatted in the street. She looked away at once.

"Idiot!" Benyoub cried out, starting to rise. "She's letting him shit in the street."

Rosie slumped in her chair.

"Look at them!"

"I don't want to," Rosie answered. "Maybe he . . ."

"As if we don't have enough trouble," Benyoub cut her off.

A waiter was coming toward their table but Benyoub waved him away apologetically. "We've changed our minds," he called.

"I thought you wanted something to eat," Rosie said.

"I only came here for you."

"Then we can walk."

They had always taken long walks when money was tight.

"That's when I'm happiest," Benyoub said bitterly. "In between places. Walking."

*R*OSIE OPENED HER EYES and stared at the armoire beside the bed, a looming burled-walnut monstrosity. Although morning light filled the bedroom, Serge slept peacefully next to her. She thought of reaching for her robe in the heap of clothes on the soiled velvet chair pushed against the foot of the armoire. Wherever space permitted, someone had set yellowing lace antimacassars on the furniture.

After two nights in Serge's mother's house Rosie was eager to return to Paris. The old mattress was soft and lumpy, and their customary room seemed airless. But it was the strain of watching her every word that bothered Rosie the most. At eighty-one, Madame Deneau had perfected a look of benign disgust that always frightened her. Heavy eyelids, thick with wrinkles, hooded the old woman's eyes so that she appeared to be dozing even when she was preparing to pounce on the next statement Rosie made, whatever it might be.

Only yesterday she had been humiliated once again after failing to appreciate Mme Deneau's offer to drive her and Serge to see Montmirail Castle, just half an hour from the village. "But we've already been there," Rosie remarked, and Mme Deneau raised her eyebrows: "How, then, do you propose to spend the day?" Montmirail it was, while Rosie consoled herself with the thought that at least they weren't going to Chambord, where on previous visits Madame had insisted on seeing every one of the four hundred rooms, or so it had seemed. Rosie had always felt intimidated by the châteaus, and took comfort in Serge's remark that they were built by Renaissance scum — the kind of men who today would be international real-estate developers.

Fifteen years ago Mme Deneau had returned from Paris to the country house where she was born. Now known as *"l'aristocrate"* in a village where her father had been mayor, Mme Deneau lived with her unmarried daughter Odile, who had recently turned sixty. After years of estrangement the two women were glued to each other. And Rosie pitied them.

Long after Odile's father had died, Madame had married Hervé Deneau, a man nine years her junior, and when Odile was in her mid-twenties she and her stepfather began an affair that lasted almost twenty years, ending with Hervé's death. Since then, Serge's half-sister had spent every day making amends. Mme Deneau, who of course knew of the affair, had often suggested that Odile marry — men were interested in her, some of them good men. But Serge claimed that Odile had been happiest when his father set her up in an apartment of her own, in a suburb of Paris, although Rosie saw nothing in the faded woman to suggest she had any good memories. Hervé's death had brought Odile and her mother together again.

Serge shifted from his back to his left side, groaning softly, and Rosie nestled against him. She wanted to open the windows wide but hated to disturb him by leaving the bed. "You need country sleep," Mme Deneau had told Serge shortly after they arrived. Mother and daughter then fell into an amiable argument about the vase of freshly cut roses Odile had put in the guest bedroom. Never sleep near cut flowers, Madame had insisted, while Odile held her ground, claiming that the rule applied only to house plants — Serge would enjoy her roses. No one ever mentioned his father, or the tensions that had driven Serge from his parents' house, to join the army, as soon as he was of age.

Still half asleep herself, Rosie let her thoughts drift back to the train ride from Paris. They had been talking about Deb's visit when, to her surprise, Serge said that Thierry had found Deb "an American type," even "a character," and had not been the least offended by her remarks.

"He doesn't know Americans," Rosie had objected. "And I wonder what he'd consider a French type?"

"Why do you dislike her so much?"

"I don't know. I get bored listening to Deb. But it's not really dislike. I can't explain it."

"You'd find things easier if you treated her as an interesting phenomenon rather than a personal affront. She's very lonely. That's why she kept telling you how easy life is in the States. She wants you to go back."

Like Rosie, Serge enjoyed analyzing people's motives, although they often disagreed. Serge, Rosie felt, was too generous in his judgments.

"There's no place to live," Rosie said intensely. "I mean no really good place. I hate the way everyone has to think that their city's the best, their country's the best, what they have is the best. Wherever they are is best — it's so arbitrary."

"Even Paris?" Serge had joked.

"You're my place. That's enough."

Serge had taken Rosie's hand, and they'd leaned against each other, silently looking out the train window. From their first trip together she had loved train rides with him.

A door slammed downstairs, then a second time, and Rosie heard voices below her window. She looked at the old wind-up alarm clock beside their bed: ten after eight. Madame and Odile claimed to be early risers, up before dawn, and the effort not to wake Serge must have made them restless.

Slowly pulling herself away from him, Rosie climbed out of bed and reached for her thin cotton robe. She had forgotten to pack slippers, and stepped into black pumps instead, hoping that Madame wouldn't see how scuffed they were. Odile would probably tell her later — she noticed everything flawed or imperfect.

The paneled stairs to the main floor were hung with old daguerreotypes of family picnics and stiff sepia portraits. Rosie avoided them, as if eye contact with Serge's dead relatives would be prying, rude. She'd never been curious about the photographs, and Serge once said that he couldn't identify most of them. Odile was the family historian.

Filled with fine heavy dark furniture, the parlor delighted her, and Rosie wished that she could spend the day there alone, reading and thinking. She envied Madame and Odile their solid walnut tables and the bureau whose drawer handles, shaped like clusters of grapes, were so highly polished they seemed to invite her touch. More recent photographs covered the bureau, but none of Serge's father.

Rosie hurried past the dining room, with its table that seated twelve, and entered the kitchen. Immediately she spotted an enamel coffeepot on the stove and turned up the gas flame. While the coffee heated she sat at the wooden kitchen table, where someone — probably Odile — had placed a china pitcher filled with pink roses. Apparently it was all right to eat near cut flowers. Cups and saucers had been left out for her and Serge.

The sunny table made Rosie stretch, catlike, and then yawn. No one was in sight, as if an uninhabited house had been set up just for her pleasure. She noticed that the pitcher's handle had been broken in two places and glued back with care. She would have liked to ask the name of the roses, but since she knew little about flowers, and nothing of gardens, the question could seem pretentious. Everything about this house was unlike her childhood home, where the women had to set up corners for themselves in the basement. Imagine Mme Deneau sewing in the basement — impossible.

"We thought you might sleep all day," Odile said, entering the kitchen. She carried a small basket of tomatoes.

"From your garden?" Rosie asked, looking at the basket.

"Of course."

"Serge always says he'd like to have a garden."

"But that's impossible in Paris." She smiled. "Ridiculous."

Odile wore an old straw hat on her glossy black hair that Rosie suspected was dyed. She had the same distinguished, frosty expression that Rosie feared in Madame.

"My brother doesn't appear to be well," Odile said and then turned to the stove. "The coffee's boiling."

Given the curious way the women in his family shared their men, Rosie felt uncomfortable when Odile referred to Serge as "my brother," and never by name. She always wanted to correct her, saying, "His name is Serge."

"It's about to boil over," Odile added.

Rosie jumped up from her chair and ran to the stove, where she reached for the handle of the coffee pot. She cried out and pulled back.

"Did you burn yourself?" Odile asked, watching, as she turned off the gas.

Rosie clasped her left hand around the fingers of her right. "Yes," she said softly. "But it's not a bad burn."

"Let me see." Odile took her hand, spreading out the fingers.

Rosie winced.

"You should have used the pot holder. Didn't you see it? I'll run some cold water. There. Just put your hand under the faucet."

Rosie felt certain that Odile was enjoying herself.

"Remember, I worked in a hospital laboratory," Odile continued, stepping away from the faucet. "I've seen my share of the sick. My brother looks jaundiced, that's what I think."

Serge had told neither Madame nor Odile about his recent stay in the hospital, and had asked Rosie not to mention it.

"Mother noticed as soon as we saw him get off the train."

"There's nothing wrong with Serge," Rosie said, annoyed. "He's just tired."

"Ah, yes," Odile said doubtfully.

Last night Madame had proclaimed the failure of Mitterand's decade-old Socialist government. She could never call herself a Socialist again, and planned to vote Communist in any election she was still alive to vote in. Odile had disagreed, appreciating the complexities of compromise, as she called them. Rosie wondered what Serge thought of his mother's announcement.

"What's going on?" Serge called from the kitchen door.

Embarrassed, Rosie waved her hand. "A little burn," she said dismissively. "It's nothing."

"She was boiling the coffee," Odile explained.

Serge laughed. "I guess I can't let you out of my sight."

He doesn't look well, Rosie thought, frightened. As he stood in the doorway, dressed in a wrinkled white shirt, its sleeves rolled to his elbows, and a pair of dark gray slacks that needed the press of an iron, she suddenly wanted to flee from the house, back to the train station, with Serge at her side. There must be a morning train to Paris.

"Take your coffee outside, the garden's beautiful this time of day," Odile suggested.

Serge headed toward the stove.

"But I'm not dressed yet," Rosie apologized.

"It doesn't matter." Odile moved the basket of tomatoes from the table to the sink. "Go out, both of you, and I'll bring the coffee on a tray."

"I don't want to trouble you," Serge said.

"You visit us rarely enough, brother, it's a pleasure to wait on you a little. And Maman is in the garden."

Serge led Rosie out the kitchen door, inquiring about her burn. Engulfed by a sweet, grassy scent, they took lawn chairs from beside the door to a sunny spot in the yard.

The dour, two-storied stone house had once been surrounded by acres of farmland, but in the last half century much of it had been sold off by succeeding generations abandoning the countryside. Several forested acres remained behind the house, and a large expanse of lawn before it.

"I don't see your mother," Rosie said, almost relieved.

Serge looked around. "She's over there."

Along the west side of the house trellised roses climbed in profusion, and Madame was bent over a bush, clipping back dead flowers.

"You'd like to live here, wouldn't you?" Rosie asked. "Or in a place like this."

"It has nothing to do with my life," he replied.

"Are you sure?"

"I couldn't stand the bickering between them. After you went up to bed last night Maman started in about Odile's recent talks with the village priest. Apparently she even takes him roses."

"What's wrong with that? You'd have to talk to someone out here or you'd go crazy."

"Maman's always been an atheist. She won't tolerate any talk of religion."

"Maybe Odile's discovering her true nature. She should meet Deb," Rosie said with a laugh. She'd always thought that Odile resembled a nun out of her habit.

"We'd better go over to Maman."

"You go by yourself," Rosie said. "I'm sure she'd rather talk to you alone."

Serge smiled, leaving Rosie to settle herself on one of the chairs. She knew it had been wrong to stay behind, but felt certain that nothing she did would make Madame like her. At least she could please herself. The sun had not yet begun to burn, so the morning still seemed green.

Rosie's summer robe opened to the middle of her thighs, and she looked at her untanned legs. They were not, she told herself, the legs of a forty-year-old; they had shape, line, unlike thickening middle-aged legs that only looked good in stockings. How wonderful it would be if no one came near her for the rest of the day. She wanted to curl up on the grass and sleep unencumbered by clothing. If no one spoke, if no one asked anything of her, she would be happy here. The day could grow hotter but she wouldn't mind.

Closing her eyes, Rosie looked up at the sun and let her mind go blank. Silver rays changed shapes on the inside of her eyelids, breaking into pale shimmering colors, blue and red and gold, like a turning kaleidoscope. With each shift of color, the shapes changed too, diamonds breaking apart, circles reforming. And then she thought of Benyoub.

Rosie opened her eyes, yawning again. The world was still green.

She hadn't thought of Benyoub since leaving Paris. Or of their pointless last meeting. "He doesn't know what he wants," Serge had suggested. "It's a shock to come back into someone's life — you feel lost because you remember a part of you that hasn't existed without that person." Rosie agreed, but she'd replied, "He's not back in my life."

Rosie shook her head, as if to clear her thoughts. The colors around her were faded, ordinary. She might as well dress for the day. Serge was standing beside Madame, probably planning some kind of outing — another château or a visit to neighbors. No one could sit still for very long, thinking of nothing.

Suddenly Rosie wished that she knew the names of all the trees, as Serge did. She could tell an oak from the shape of its leaves, for a huge one had stood in the middle of her backyard in Pittsburgh. The trees around Mme Deneau's weren't oak; Rosie knew that much. The summer after she'd met Serge, when they made the first of their visits to his mother, they had walked deep into the woods behind the house, until Rosie felt certain they must be lost. Then they made love on a ground cover of moss and dead leaves while Rosie looked up at the trees, trying to catch a glimpse of sky, although the dense growth blocked out the sun. As Serge moved over her, she kept waiting for someone to interrupt them, fearing that they weren't alone. At dinner that evening she'd sensed that Madame knew what she and Serge had done in the woods. A neighbor might have seen them, and told her, although it was difficult to imagine anyone telling Madame about a couple, half undressed, caressing in her woods. "We are a cruel and tribal people," Madame was saying to Serge and Odile, about some politician's recent speech. She knows, Rosie had decided. As a boy, hadn't Serge often gone into the woods to read, once even leaving a book there, a worn copy of *The Aeneid*? Madame, of course, would never say a word about the afternoon to her son, or to Rosie. But she had other ways of letting you know her disapproval. After dinner she'd taken Rosie's hand and said, "Let me show you the bats." Rosie had turned to Serge. "We're in the country," he'd said. So she had to follow Mme Deneau out onto the lawn, where a moody late twilight made the woods seem closer to the house than they had appeared in daylight. *"Regardez!"* the old woman pointed, and Rosie watched something swoop down near the eaves of the house. Then she saw another, and another. She tried not to shudder — she had never seen a live bat before. Madame was getting even.

As Odile came marching across the lawn Rosie drew her robe together. "Serge is with your mother," she called.

"Yes, yes," Odile said, setting the tray on the grass. "I couldn't carry a table at the same time."

"We don't need one," Rosie said, thanking her for bringing the coffee. "You've already done too much for us."

Odile looked at the tray. "As you like." Then, heading back to the house, she waved at Serge, who was crossing the lawn to join Rosie.

"What happened to your mother?" Rosie asked.

"She's gone inside. You should have come over."

Rosie ignored his remark. "What's being planned?" she asked.

"A visit with cousins. I haven't seen them for ten years at least."

"Oh, God," she sighed. "Are you up to it? How are you feeling?"

"I'm fine." He sat beside her, bending for a cup.

"That's not what Odile thinks. Or your mother. How are you really?"

"What did Odile tell you?"

"Only that you look jaundiced. So I said you were well. But you aren't, are you?"

Serge began pouring the coffee.

"Why won't you tell me what's going on?" Rosie asked.

"I'm planning to see the doctor when we get back to Paris. For more tests."

"What kind of tests? I thought that's what they were doing while you were in the hospital."

"You know how doctors are, they'll test forever."

"You and Odile drank a lot of wine at dinner last night."

Serge took a sip of his coffee. "Not really."

"Three bottles."

"Rosie, don't start getting judgmental."

"Life means judging things. At least I'm ready to discuss the basis of my opinions."

Serge shook his head. "What's got into you? And this early in the day."

"Maybe the country air." She laughed. "But your mother never finished her first glass, I saw that, and I only had a couple of glasses, so you and Odile drank the rest. That's a lot of wine for someone having trouble with his liver."

"I've cut back, you see that."

"Even so, I don't want you to be sick. You're too important to me."

Serge was about to reply but she stopped him. "If you won't watch out for yourself, then do it for me."

10

Rosie and Serge left Madame Deneau's with a string bag full of fresh vegetables, which gave Rosie an idea. In the days before he went into the hospital she vowed to make all of the foods Serge loved even though he claimed little appetite. Steamed mussels, beefsteak tartare, kidneys in mustard sauce with boiled potatoes. She seemed always to be stopping at the Monoprix for one last ingredient.

"You haven't cooked like this for years," he said, watching her spread goat cheese on croutons for their salad. "I should get sick more often."

"Don't joke about that. You're getting better, aren't you?"

"Of course I am. Can't you see?"

Although she feared the question sounded like a child's, Rosie kept asking Serge if he felt better. She had canceled her classes the next morning in order to accompany him to the hospital.

"Odile seemed worried about you. She said you looked jaundiced."

"Why do you listen to her? I thought you didn't even like Odile."

"She worked in a medical lab, Serge, she knows more than I do."

"She's not a doctor. Anyone can see I'm getting better."

"But you've never really explained what's been wrong. Every time I ask . . ."

"It's a little liver problem, Rosie . . ."

". . . you cut me off just like that. I'm not your pet."

"I don't mean to. But forget Odile," he paused, taking a sip of wine. "I remember when I was fourteen and I went to the movies with my father, and she'd decide to come along. I sensed something was going on, the way they sat beside each other."

Rosie joined Serge at the table, with the salad. He seemed weary, and she feared he had lost more weight. How do you tell when someone has jaundice? She wished Odile had explained.

"They never touched, at least not in front of me. But I think I knew they wanted to. And I resented it."

"Do you still resent her?"

"Not any more. It's like you and Deb — we'll never be close, not like some families."

"Families," Rosie sighed.

"Do you hate Deb as much as it seems?"

"It's not hate. It's just that we can't talk about anything important. Even when we were kids we rarely played together, though my parents wanted us to."

"No one expected that of me and Odile," Serge said. "The age difference made her one of the grownups, not really a sister."

"You were lucky. With Deb, our animosity just grew and grew. Something about her always made me mad. And I guess she felt the same about me. I never know what will set her off. One of the women at school — she's from Montreal — told a story today about Isaac Singer, and I thought I'd write Deb, since she's so obsessed with him, but then I wondered if she'd really want to hear that when he lectured in Montreal he kept asking people where he could buy inexpensive beaver hats. I might be stepping onto a minefield, you know."

"Poor Deb," Serge said with a laugh.

"Poor Deb?"

"She tries so hard to be serious but she's not very bright. There's something stunted about her."

"When I was about twelve, I wanted a bottle of Evening in Paris cologne. They sold it at Woolworth's, in a beautiful little blue-glass bottle — it seemed so grownup — and finally my mother bought it for my birthday. But Deb couldn't stand that I had something I wanted so badly, so she asked to use it too and managed to spill most of the cologne on my bedroom floor. It stank for weeks."

"That's just what I meant," Serge said. "She's like some suspicious old peasant who thinks the world's out to cheat her."

"She was born that way," Rosie laughed. "And what am I like?"

"You must be the world that wants to do the cheating." He took her hand tenderly.

"I wished you hadn't asked Thierry and Renée over tonight."

"They won't stay long."

"You look tired, Serge. I know you're worrying."

He shrugged. "You've gone to all this trouble and I'm not very hungry."

"Neither am I," Rosie said, helping herself to the salad. "But you have to eat something."

Serge refilled his wine glass while Rosie stared at her plate.

"They're probably going to tell you to give up drinking," she finally said.

"I suppose so."

They ate in silence, Serge picking at his meal. Although the appliances were old, and the kitchen had been wallpapered with an unfortunate floral pattern, the room was a place of comfort, with the copper pots and pans that Serge had bought for Rosie in her cooking days, after they decided to live together. Now she used the bright kettle on top of the refrigerator to hold a bunch of dried hydrangeas — the lid had misplaced itself somewhere. Though the kitchen was actually too crowded, Rosie liked eating there with Serge. But tonight she hadn't bothered to light candles. On the wall beside the table hung a framed fin-de-siècle poster, one of Lautrec's dancer-prostitutes. Rosie thought of it as Paris kitsch but never said so to Serge, who claimed that the person who gave him the poster had said it was an original. In the apartment across the courtyard opera was playing too loudly. Rosie had heard the music many times but couldn't identify it. They were still lingering at the table when someone knocked at the door.

"Here already?" Rosie said absently.

"I'll go," Serge offered, pushing back his chair.

"I'll clean up later, but I should put a few things away now."

Serge disappeared for a moment but soon returned to the kitchen.

"The coffee's on," Rosie said from the sink, spooning leftovers into a plastic carton.

"Benyoub is here."

"I don't believe it."

"See for yourself."

Instead of turning to the doorway, she put down a plate with a thud. "Do you know what he wants?"

"I didn't ask."

From his tone of voice she couldn't tell what was going through Serge's mind.

"Bring him in," she sighed.

As Benyoub stepped into the kitchen, wearing one of his perfectly ironed white shirts, Rosie heard another knock on the door.

"We're having company," she explained.

"Did I come at a bad time? I'm sorry." He pressed his lips together.

"We've just finished dinner."

He stood silently as she rinsed a bowl. "I'm sorry," he repeated.

"Have you eaten?" she asked.

"I'm not hungry."

"What is this? Nobody's hungry any more." Suddenly she felt light-headed. Introducing Benyoub to the Roussels wouldn't be as gruesome as introducing Deb.

"Are we too early?" Renée appeared at the kitchen door. "I told Thierry . . ."

"Of course not," Rosie replied, watching Benyoub turn to Renée and flash one of his unpredictable wide smiles. Renée, off guard, seemed charmed, and Rosie remembered that Hamed had once gone with older married women for money. Had Ben done that too?

"I'm a friend of Rosie's," he said.

"This is Benyoub," Rosie added.

Renée looked confused, as if somehow Rosie had moved up a notch in her opinion. Tonight she'd tied around her head a yellow silk scarf with a pattern that appeared to be small black footprints.

Serge and Thierry now stood at the doorway, looking in.

"Serge, will you do the introductions while I get the coffee?" Rosie tried not to laugh to herself: as if I have so many secrets.

"Can I help you?" Ben offered.

"Everyone out of my kitchen," she said brightly. "Out."

"We'd better listen to her," said Serge, feigning fear.

Alone, Rosie felt the curious pleasure of standing to the side, waiting to join her own party. It seemed almost perverse to her, but she didn't want to give it up. And to her surprise she felt amused — even glad — that Benyoub had shown up. She suspected that Serge, who loved crowds, didn't mind.

Setting cups and saucers on a wooden tray, she listened as the voices in the living room joined the soprano from across the courtyard. Of course Serge would get everyone talking amiably. When he finished with all these tests she really ought to give a big party for him; he would like that. But what did Benyoub want? With the Roussels around at least he couldn't ask to borrow more money.

"I've always wanted to see Algeria," Renée was saying as Rosie entered the living room. "Especially the desert."

Rosie thought of all the old needlework that had so far been safe from Renée.

"I have too," Thierry added. "I went to Morocco once. Years ago, at Christmas."

"Before you knew me," Renée said.

"Before then."

"But you've been," Renée said to Rosie. "Benyoub was just telling us."

"That was in my Arab phase. I would have been glad to be taken for an Algerian."

Did Ben frown? He was not as dark as Hamed, and now Rosie remembered his confession that when he first came to Paris he'd tried to pass for French.

"We went far enough south to see the desert," Benyoub said.

Rosie set the tray on a table before the sofa. "It was a mass of color — ochre and violet and deep red and gray —

all vibrating . . . the oasis at Bou Saada. About 150 miles from Algiers. I wanted to drive but Ben wouldn't let me."

"You're a terrible driver."

"And I bought a fan made from embroidered palm leaves. I must have it in a drawer somewhere."

"We should go," Renée said, lighting a cigarette.

"There's probably a McDonald's on every corner now," Rosie suggested.

"No there isn't," Benyoub said.

"I remember being surprised that one of the main streets in Algiers was called Avenue Franklin Roosevelt."

"You can't escape America anywhere," Serge said.

"Algeria's different from Morocco," Benyoub said, declining Rosie's offer of coffee with a shake of his head. "I hate it when people lump all of North Africa together and call it *Maghreb*. Algeria's rougher than Morocco. Purer."

"I'd like that," Renée said.

"How do you mean, purer?" Thierry asked.

"You want tea, Ben?" Rosie asked. "I've even got mint, and chamomile."

"No thank you."

In a minute they'll be onto the ins and outs of Algerian politics, Rosie thought, but Benyoub was in safe company. Such talk might even be the best thing to distract Serge. Thierry looked ready for any kind of discussion, and Rosie prepared to be amazed at all that he probably knew about Algeria. She gave him five minutes to bring up collectivization and agriculture. Ben had always been good company when he wanted. Now he was talking of immigrants who had no intention of assimilating, who no longer wanted to fit in, and of his old anger at the French for making him feel inferior, an outsider.

"I'm going to open some wine," Serge said, without moving.

"Not for me," Renée said, reaching for a cup of coffee. Rosie caught her eye and Renée smiled.

"I'll have some," Thierry said.

Serge went into the kitchen while Rosie sat on the sofa beside Benyoub, who had clasped his hands like an Old Testament god about to pass judgment. She felt angry at Thierry and Serge. The coffee was fresh, it should have been enough.

"Do you know anything about the Algerian film industry?" Renée asked, offering Benyoub a cigarette.

He shook his head at the package.

"I write film reviews for *L'Humanité,*" she explained.

Rosie looked into her coffee cup. The desert, she recalled, had frightened her.

"But I don't think I've ever reviewed anything Algerian."

"Yes you did," Thierry corrected. "A couple years ago you . . ."

A loud crash in the kitchen startled everyone.

"Serge?" Rosie called. "What happened?"

No reply.

Rosie jumped up, spilling coffee on her skirt. "Oh shit," she muttered.

Thierry held out a napkin but Rosie ran into the kitchen, where Serge stood leaning against the sink, several broken plates on the floor at his feet.

"Serge?" she cried.

He didn't turn.

"What's wrong?"

He was retching into the sink, making horrible noises, gasping for air.

Rosie stood beside him. She put her hand on his back.

"What is it?" Thierry asked from the doorway.

"He's vomiting blood!" Rosie cried.

Serge grabbed onto the edge of the sink, and Thierry reached to hold him up.

"He's vomiting blood," she repeated.

"Lean on me," Thierry said to Serge. "I'm right here, I'm holding onto you."

As Rosie reached across the sink to turn on the water tap, she saw blood streaked over the front of Serge's shirt. Renée and Benyoub stood watching Serge.

"You should call an ambulance," Thierry said.

"Do something!" Rosie said.

Benyoub left the doorway and went to the telephone.

"How much did you drink?" Thierry asked.

"He didn't drink much," Rosie said protectively.

There were dark red patches on Serge's neck and cheeks.

"It's an allergic reaction," she suggested.

Renée followed Benyoub.

"How much did he drink?" Thierry asked again.

"I don't know, maybe half a bottle. Not a lot," Rosie said. "But he didn't eat much."

"Is anyone calling an ambulance?" Thierry asked.

The kitchen now stank, and Rosie put her arms around Serge. "Do you want to lie down?"

"Just get him a chair."

Rosie stared blankly at Thierry.

"From the table over there."

She let go of Serge and dragged a chair to him.

"You're heavier than you look," Thierry said as he pulled Serge onto the chair. "You'll be fine. There, lean back."

"Can't you talk?" Rosie asked, holding Serge by his shoulders.

"There's an ambulance coming," Renée said, joining them. "Benyoub called."

Serge leaned forward, his head in his hands.

"Do you need to throw up again?" Thierry asked.

"No," he replied. "I'm sorry."

Renée knelt beside him. "We'll take you into the hospital tonight instead of tomorrow morning. We'll all go."

"He'll be all right?" Rosie said to Thierry, who seemed not to hear.

"Are you in pain?" Renée asked.

"My stomach. Everything. My insides."

Benyoub returned to the kitchen. "They said to cover him with a blanket in case he's in shock."

"He's not in shock," Rosie said.

"I don't know," Thierry said.

"Are you cold?" Rosie encircled Serge with her arms. "Are you okay?"

He nodded. "I'm better now."

"Renée, would you find him a sweater? Or a jacket?"

"I'm not cold," Serge replied.

"Your hands are shaking," Rosie said.

"It's just nerves," he said.

"The ambulance won't be long," said Benyoub.

"Just nerves," repeated Serge. "I'll be fine."

11

$\mathcal{A}$FTER HIS FIRST NIGHT in a hospital ward, Serge was transferred to a private room. Though preferable, it still seemed ominous to Rosie. When she finally saw the doctor who had admitted Serge, she approached him gingerly. In his late thirties, he now wore a tailored blue dress shirt with a white collar and a white necktie — the kind of clothes that she imagined cost enough to feed a small family for a week.

"Are you his wife?" he asked as she stopped him outside of Serge's room.

How had he guessed she wasn't? "No," she began, "but . . ."

"You know him well?"

"We live together." Surely it was none of his business. He seemed to be studying her, as if she were difficult to classify. Of course he would know that she wasn't French.

"He's very sick."

The doctor's eyes never met hers.

"What?" Rosie exclaimed.

"He's a very sick man."

"I don't understand. What's wrong with him? He's never been sick before."

"Alcoholic hepatitis," he said.

Rosie looked down at the floor. Its faded linoleum squares seemed as ominous as the private room.

"You know he has cirrhosis of the liver? From alcohol."

"But he's not an alcoholic," she blurted out. "He doesn't drink that much."

"He's very sick, Madame, what else can I say? But we're watching him closely. We're giving him the best possible care."

Does he think I'm going to sue him? Rosie wondered, as if all Americans carried a list of lawyers to phone in any emergency.

"What is his blood pressure?"

"There's nothing wrong with his blood pressure, Madame. He's bleeding, but not enough to affect his blood pressure."

"I don't think I know your name," she said, staring into his face.

"Dr. Bernard Chollet."

"Dr. Bernard Chollet," she repeated. "Yes."

"I'm afraid I can't talk with you now," he said.

"Of course," she replied, suddenly afraid that he might somehow punish Serge if he disliked her. "When can you talk with me?"

"Another time, Madame. Later."

If only Thierry had been with her, or even Renée. Better yet, Serge, when he was well.

Dr. Chollet turned on his heel in a style that Rosie thought had been much practiced, and she watched him disappear down the quiet corridor.

In his room Serge appeared to be sleeping. With a tube in his left nostril, and an intravenous needle in his left arm, he looked every bit as sick as the doctor had claimed. Rosie put her purse on a metal chair by the window and drew another chair to his bedside.

Little sunlight came in through the window from a small, well-lit courtyard — it might be February outside, not August — and the impersonal room seemed to emphasize the seriousness of Serge's condition. Rosie looked at him; he appeared to be breathing easily, despite the grim tube in his nose. The circles under his eyes seemed darker, even swollen, while his face had taken on an unpleasant bronze cast. Or, Rosie thought, maybe it was just the pale yellow sheets making his complexion seem darker.

Thirsty, she wished that she'd brought along a can of fruit juice, or a soft drink, in her bag. The bright blue plastic container on the formica-topped bedside table must have held water, but it looked too sinister to touch.

Was Serge's odd color from jaundice? She would have to ask the doctor. "Are you sleeping, Serge?" she whispered.

He didn't reply, and she listened to his breathing.

"I'm here now. But you don't have to wake up. I'm not going any place."

A small pile of magazines and newspapers, folded in half, nearly covered the bedside table. Thierry must have brought them yesterday. Then Rosie noticed a copy of *Eugénie Grandet*. Someone had left that too. She never remembered Serge mentioning Balzac. Why would anyone think a person sick enough to be in the hospital would feel overcome with an urge to read the classics? She reached for the book, which she had always meant to read, and thumbed through its pages without actually taking in the words.

Rosie had always dreaded August — the end of summer meant the start of a new school year, the coming High Holidays, with endless family dinners run by Uncle Aladar and Aunt Pearl, and, since she'd lived in Paris, a city overrun by tourists, while all the French who could fled for the country. Though some poet had mistaken April for the cruelest month, it had to be August, if you were limited to only one choice; but every month was the cruelest month.

Rosie put the book aside and reached for a *Paris Match,* the kind of magazine Serge never touched, when she noticed that he'd been watching her. "Are you all right?" she asked.

"What were you thinking about?" he replied.

"Nothing important." Was it possible that the whites of his eyes were yellow?

"No. Tell me. You looked so serious."

"Well, it's silly, but I was remembering the end of summer and how my mother would take me downtown on the bus to buy new clothes for school, and I would hold her hand while we crossed the street, even when I was a teenager, because the traffic frightened her. She always thought a car might jump onto the sidewalk and run us down."

Serge smiled.

"I told you it was silly."

"But it's not. That's a sweet memory."

"I felt responsible for my mother, I don't know if that's sweet. Now tell me what's been happening here all day."

He closed his eyes for a moment. "Just more tests. You didn't phone Odile, I hope. Or Maman."

"No."

"Good. I don't want them to visit, that's the last thing I can face now."

"If that's what you want, Serge." Rosie set the magazine on the table and drew her chair closer to the bed. "What does the doctor say?"

"Well, for a start, that I can never touch liquor again."

"But you don't drink all that much."

"That's what I told him. But apparently my liver's shot."

"You're going to get better."

"I'm so tired, I only want to sleep."

"Maybe it's the medication they're giving you."

"That's what Ben said."

"Benyoub?"

"He was here. A little while ago."

"What did he want?"

"He left some magazines. I think he's lonely."

Rosie reached for his hand.

"He said he'd be back."

"I'm sorry he's bothering you."

"I don't mind, really. He's rather innocent."

"Oh, God, Serge, I just can't trust him. He has to want something."

"He said he was worried about me."

"He never worries about anyone but himself. Not really."

"Are you sure? We talked about Algeria. It got my mind off things for a while."

"Let's not discuss him. Why don't you sleep now? You look tired."

"Promise me something?"

"What?" she asked.

"Don't worry about me. Go home and have supper. I just need to rest."

Careful of the tubes, Rosie leaned forward to kiss his lips. "I'll see you tomorrow," she whispered.

"And the day after," he said.

"Of course you will."

"Go have some supper now, and write to your sister."

Why, Rosie wondered as she left Serge, would he want her to write to Deb? But she'd been right about his health, after all. Poor old Deb. Would it give her some satisfaction to know she'd been right? Rosie didn't feel up to that. Surely if everyone said Serge would be better, and if they meant it, then he'd be fine. Doctors had medicines for practically everything nowadays. And people lived happy lives without a drop of liquor. Serge would get well, and Rosie promised herself to take better care of him.

In the days that followed Rosie visited the hospital nightly, after work, and Thierry or Renée usually joined her there. Serge rarely left his bed, and still had no appetite — untouched bowls of soup or yogurt often remained on the bedside table. Perhaps she should bring him something to eat from home, something he'd really like. He looked pitifully thin, but his feet and ankles were swollen. And he often seemed confused, even forgetting that Deb had already gone back to New York. He read a bit, he told Rosie, but had trouble concentrating. Mostly he slept.

After one visit Rosie turned to Thierry and said, "He's not getting better, is he? He's getting worse."

They left Serge's room in silence, and headed to the subway. Outside, the light from the hospital illuminated a dull summer sky. Thierry took Rosie's arm as they walked. "I spoke to the head of the department," he began. "And he thinks that Serge will recover. But it's serious."

"I just don't understand. The day before he got sick he was out on the street selling newspapers, the same as always. And then he's vomiting blood."

"He's been sick a long time, Rosie. Longer than you know."

"What do you mean?"

"Before you met him, I guess it was in '79, he went into the hospital. It was a kind of nervous breakdown. And he was having liver trouble then."

"No one told me this before."

"When the two of you got together Serge drank a lot less, we were all grateful to you."

"You said a nervous breakdown?"

"Serge is more fragile than you think. He always has been."

Rosie pulled her arm away from Thierry. The conversation made her feel as if she were betraying Serge.

"He's a lot like his father."

"I don't know what you're suggesting. I know his father was a Communist, but . . ."

"That's not what I mean. You know about Odile?"

"Yes."

"Serge's father was very weak. Charming, but weak. You know I love Serge, he's my best friend, he's closer than a brother, but I know him well. Life's too much for him. I don't think he'll ever hold a job again, maybe something part-time, but you have to accept that, Rosie. You have to be prepared."

"He's fifty-two years old, for God's sake, how can you say that?"

"I told you I spoke with his doctor. Serge has been ill for years, and it's going to take a long time for him to recover."

"I don't like this conversation."

"I understand. But I have one more thing to say."

"What is it?" Rosie asked warily.

"You should tell his family what's happened."

"But he asked me not to. In fact, he insisted."

"What if he doesn't get better?"

"You just said he's going to be fine, the doctor told you . . ."

"I don't know, Rosie, but if he can, he will. He loves you very much."

"Do you know something you're not telling me?"

"No," Thierry said, taking her arm again. "But think about phoning Madame Deneau. I don't want to upset you, but please think about it."

Rosie nodded. Nothing was going as it should. Nothing was getting better. And it wasn't fair. Other people got married, bought houses, took wonderful vacations, lived happily. Other people were lucky.

At the entrance to the Métro, where they would take trains in different directions, Thierry offered to accompany Rosie home.

"No, you'd better go on, it's late. And Renée's waiting. I'm fine." She turned her cheek for him to kiss. "Really."

"You know you can call us anytime."

Rosie hurried down the subway steps without looking back to wave, and for a moment she feared that Thierry had followed her. She didn't want to hear another word from him, not tonight. Such male sentimentality — the thought that he needed to see her home! She only wanted time to think.

The idea of Serge having a nervous breakdown struck her as preposterous. What could Thierry have meant? The phrase itself seemed melodramatic. A breakdown. Serge had always been strong, and encouraging; in control. He was the person people came to for help. Surely Thierry had misunderstood.

Serge wasn't like other men, he always clipped articles for her to read, noted passages in books, shared a favorite chanson. He had a huge collection of French songs, not only Piaf and Greco but Brassens, Ferré, Bécaud, and Béart, and he played them over and over until Rosie had come to anticipate every breath each singer took. In the last decade, as they were heard less frequently on the radio, Serge often railed at the rock music that had taken their place. "But America must be heard," he'd say with sarcasm, and Rosie, of course, agreed. Serge belonged to a France that was dying, to the movies of Bresson and the poems of Prévert; he still cared about the International Brigade. If Thierry was his best friend, he had to know that.

Rosie usually found that thinking of Serge's virtues had a calming effect on her. But not tonight. She knew that she and Serge weren't blind to each other's defects. Didn't he often warn her not to be too critical of people, of herself? He teased her when she ignored his advice, mocked her moods of "injured goodness," as he called them, said that rancor was self-defeating. And he did all of this while they wandered through the city, visited cathedrals, examined old relics. How odd, when she thought of it, that this Communist who had no time for modern buildings was drawn to cathedrals.

He had to get well. He couldn't die. She had already buried her parents — that was enough. Although she could hardly remember her mother's funeral. There had been some kind of argument between Deb and her father, yes, but its subject had faded. She only remembered the embarrassment Aunt Pearl seemed to feel over the circumstances of Elza's death, as if her mother had deprived the family of a chance to suffer nobly through a long, drawn-out illness.

There were so many things Rosie couldn't remember. She thought of the old passport photograph of Elza as a young woman, taken in Budapest just after the war, which Serge had put into a small morocco leather frame found in some flea market during one of their summer vacations — which one? To Spain? Probably. Whenever she thought of her mother she saw the face in that photograph, and not a face in her memory. The mind seemed intent on its own loyalties. If it hadn't been for Serge, she might have misplaced the photograph: a young woman in a dark felt hat pulled forward over her brow, looked directly into the camera, as if she didn't see it. Yet her expression had nothing to do with self-confidence. The young girl, like the camera, seemed not to exist.

Elza had never mentioned death or dying, and neither had Serge. The thought made Rosie shudder, even though she found the idea of her own death comforting. As long as it wasn't painful, death meant the end of wanting and needing, of all limitations. It was only the thought of other people's deaths that frightened her.

Leaving the subway, Rosie headed for a small North African restaurant that she and Serge liked and pushed her way through the long strings of black and white plastic beads hanging inside the door. She wasn't ready to face the empty apartment alone. After ten o'clock, most of the tables were empty except for several groups of elderly men. Still, any restaurant was better than sitting by herself and listening to Serge's records, as if he were just out at a meeting and due home any minute. She might even write to Deb after all. Since Rosie's first years in Paris she had loved sitting in restaurants while writing letters home, but tonight she had nothing to tell anyone.

An unfamiliar elderly waiter across the room stood watching her, but she didn't reach for a menu. Couldn't she just sit here for a while? "They have to make a living too," Serge might have said. A philodendron vine grew twenty feet along the wall, from a pot in the window that had been wrapped in aluminum foil. Beside the pot were bowls of lemons and tomatoes, and a tray of almond pastry. Someone had randomly stuck postcards on the walls.

Rosie searched through her canvas bag for a pen, wishing that she could empty it on the table and sort out its contents. People were so uptight about things like that. After cleaning the bag she might go into the kitchen, wash her hair in the sink with the new shampoo she'd been given, and ask for a towel before returning to her table to dry her hair. Then she might like an espresso. Maybe even some couscous.

"Rosie."

She looked up to find Benyoub.

"You work here?" she asked.

"No," he said. "I was looking for you."

She saw no way to escape him.

"I went to your apartment and waited awhile, and then decided to go home. If you hadn't been at this window table I wouldn't have seen you."

"Sit down then. I don't know why I'm here. I'm not really hungry, but I didn't want to go home yet."

Benyoub sat across from her. "Did you see Serge tonight?"

"Of course. I just came from him."

"How is he?"

Rosie felt too tired to resent his question. "I don't know," she said. "I forgot to ask about his blood pressure."

"He's looking better," Benyoub offered.

"You think so? He looks worse to me. That's what I told Thierry."

"I like your friends."

Rosie nodded dismissively. "You really think he's going to be okay?"

Benyoub put his elbows on the table.

"You don't have to answer that," Rosie said with a sigh. "I'm probably driving everyone crazy, asking it over and over, but I can't help myself."

"You love Serge very much."

Rosie thought she was going to cry.

"I can tell," he added. "But Renée and Thierry don't love each other."

"Who told you that?"

"No one. But I can see it."

"Love's not that simple, Ben. Did Renée say something? Or Thierry?" It seemed peculiar to be discussing them with Benyoub.

"I just paid attention to how they acted. I don't care if they love each other or not, I still like them."

"They're the last people on earth I would have thought you'd like."

Benyoub stared down at his hands. "You're just saying that."

"No I'm not. You know I don't just say things. I can see why you'd like Serge but . . ."

"You don't like them, do you?"

"I like Thierry a lot."

Benyoub laughed.

"Well I do."

"Okay, okay. You don't owe me an explanation."

"No," she shrugged.

"But you don't like Renée."

Now Rosie laughed too. "All right. Have it your way. Why were you looking for me?"

"I was worried about you."

"I'll be fine." He knew her better than she wanted to admit. "Is there something you want, Ben?"

He frowned, apparently offended.

"Why do I have to want something to visit you? I just thought you might like some company, what with Serge in the hospital."

Rosie looked into his face. Perhaps all this attention was a matter of pride: he couldn't borrow money from her without believing that he belonged in her life. Or maybe his life was temporarily empty, and he needed a place to rest. Or, or . . . she could get lost imagining reasons for Ben's actions and never come close. His words, tonight, sounded direct, sincere. Once again she felt like crying.

"You don't need to hide from me," Benyoub said.

"I'm not hiding, Ben. I'm worried about Serge."

"I know you love Serge, but I wonder if you're really happy."

Rosie hadn't expected such a remark. "I'm not happy," she once told her father, before moving to Paris, and he replied, "Grownups don't think about happiness."

Across the room the waiter pushed several chairs into place at their tables, and Rosie reached for the menu, a photocopied page pasted onto a piece of cardboard. "I'd better order something. I have an early class tomorrow."

"Are you happy with your life?"

"What a question!"

"You don't have to answer me," Benyoub said. "But it's worth thinking about."

"Why are you asking that now? Why now? When I'm down."

"Can't you see how sick Serge is?"

"I won't hear that — not from you. You're not a doctor. What do you know?"

"You're always hiding, Rosie."

"Get out of here! Get out! I didn't ask you to come here. I didn't ask you for anything."

Quietly Benyoub got up and left the restaurant.

12

ROSIE SAT IN A SMALL, windowless office in the hospital, several floors below Serge's room, her hands folded in her lap, as Dr. Simone Bertin, a small, dark Corsican with a dry manner, explained that Serge had recently developed a problem with his esophagus. He had also caught a cold with a bad cough. It seemed to be more than a cold to Rosie.

"He's very dependent, you know," Dr. Bertin was saying.

Medical details were beyond Rosie. Why couldn't the doctors do something to help Serge? Other people went to the hospital and got well.

"What do you mean by 'dependent'?" Rosie asked, watching as Dr. Bertin thrust out her chin like a stubborn child. She had thick black hair that Rosie admired.

"We had a psychiatrist examine him too," Dr. Bertin continued. "He also found Monsieur Deneau to be very dependent."

"That makes him sound like just another sad case," Rosie said.

Dr. Bertin stiffened imperceptibly. "Excuse me?"

"Never mind," Rosie replied. "My nerves are bad, I've

been under a lot of stress. But what do you mean by dependent? He takes care of himself."

"A dependent personality."

Rosie thought of asking a third time, then decided that this serious-minded doctor would never explain. She wondered if Dr. Bertin — her hands were ringless — had a husband and family. How many children? Although a white lab coat covered her dress, Rosie had noticed the beige hem of her skirt beneath it.

"What's his blood pressure?" Rosie asked.

"That is not the problem," Dr. Bertin answered.

"He's getting worse, isn't he?"

"He's not getting better yet. But I think he will, in time. These things move slowly, Mme Deneau."

Rosie smiled to herself. At least somebody saw that she mattered to Serge, that she had a right to know about his health. "He's been here almost a month. You think he's going to get better."

"We're doing everything possible."

"But he didn't have a cold when he came to the hospital." She wanted to ask about internal bleeding but couldn't get the words out.

"He's a very weak man, Madame."

They left it at that, and Rosie returned to Serge's room as confused as ever. Dr. Bertin may have meant to be reassuring, but Rosie still didn't understand why Serge was getting worse. Anyone could see that he now had problems breathing, that sometimes he gasped for air. His color had improved, as Renée had been the first to note — he certainly looked less jaundiced — but no one could say he was getting better. While his arms were thinner, his abdomen had grown, gradually at first, but over a week it had bloated into a firm, tense hump. Thierry had again suggested telephoning Mme Deneau or Odile, but Serge brushed the idea aside.

Rosie would only do as he asked. Instead, she talked about her students, trying to entertain Serge with the kind of details that he usually enjoyed. And as she talked she found herself coming up with an anecdote from every day's work, which made her dislike the repetition in her job a little less. When she felt too tired to amuse him with stories, she read aloud. They had finished *Eugénie Grandet* and begun *Père Goriot*, perfect hospital books, she decided, because they moved along briskly. She wasn't certain if Serge always listened, or listened very carefully, but wouldn't ask. At least, she told herself, I'm better than a radio.

Fortunately Serge had visitors, people from the newspaper, from the party's office, from the neighborhood, people Serge had once helped. Rosie warned them not to stay very long but urged everyone to return. "See how much you matter," she often reminded Serge as he slept. "You've got to get well." Did he hear? She wanted him to know that people depended on him.

Several days after her conversation with Simone Bertin, Rosie was detained by a union meeting at school, and she arrived at the hospital later than usual. She hurried to Serge's room, and found the door was closed. This had never happened before; even when patients were sleeping their doors remained open. She knocked softly and then turned the knob, opening the door onto an empty room. It smelled strongly of disinfectant.

Rosie caught her panic and for a moment forgot the way to the nurses' station. It was almost eight o'clock and visitors were already leaving the hospital. Along the corridor to the left, she thought, beyond the elevator, looking into the empty room a final time. Magazines and books no longer covered the night table, as if Serge had never been there. The bed had been stripped of sheets and left bare. Those hideous pale-yellow sheets.

Before Rosie had the chance to turn, a nurse came out of the room next to her, carrying a plastic tray of medication, and motioned her aside. "Monsieur Deneau has been moved," she explained.

It was the night nurse, a handsome young black woman from Martinique whom Rosie liked. Her face and voice were gentle, sympathetic, like her soft island accent, and she'd never been impatient with Serge.

"Why?" Rosie asked.

"They've taken him to intensive care."

Rosie stood dazed, motionless.

"On the third floor."

"Is something wrong?" Her voice seemed to be coming from another person.

"He wasn't here went I came on shift tonight. I'd go down with you but I can't leave the floor, they don't like that. Just take the elevator. You'll find him."

"Yesterday he ate a whole carton of yogurt," Rosie said. "Isn't that a good sign? He's all right, isn't he?"

The nurse patted her arm, which only increased Rosie's panic.

On the third floor Rosie immediately went to the main desk, where a stocky middle-aged woman with short brown hair sat reading a patient's chart.

"Monsieur Deneau, Serge Deneau, can you tell me where he is?" Rosie asked, approaching. "I have to see him."

The nurse looked up slowly. She had a large reddish mole near her lower lip. "Yes?"

"Serge Deneau, he's been moved down here, from the fifth floor, they told me to come to the third floor."

"This is intensive care, Madame."

"I know that. Serge Deneau. D-E-N-E-A-U," she spelled out the name.

"Yes, Madame, you'll have to speak to his doctor."

"But he's here, right?"

"Who, Madame?"

"Serge Deneau."

"Yes, he's here. He was brought in this afternoon. But you have to see his doctor, Madame. We aren't allowed to report on a patient."

"Why not, for God's sake?"

"I'm sorry, Madame."

Rosie looked about. She was alone with the nurse, who held the chart in her left hand, a pencil in her right. A bouquet of out-of-season Parma violets stood in a small glass near her telephone.

"Please, can't you tell me anything?"

"I'm very sorry, really, but you have to speak with his doctor. I suggest you telephone him in the morning."

"In the morning!" cried Rosie. "This is crazy. I'm not leaving until I speak to someone."

The nurse shrugged.

"What's your name?" Rosie asked angrily.

"My name, Madame?"

"Yes, that's what I said." Uncle Aladar had always advised, "Get their names — it puts 'em on edge."

"Hélène Sylvère," she said. "I'm only following hospital rules."

"Do you know where I can reach Dr. Chollet? Or Dr. Bertin?"

"Not at this hour."

"Then I'm going to sit over there and wait for a doctor, I don't care if it takes all night."

"Madame? We don't have chairs for visitors."

"Then I'll sit on the floor right by the elevator until I can talk with a doctor."

Rosie stepped away from the desk while Hélène Sylvère glared at her, and then she chose a spot along the opposite wall, six feet from the elevator. Fortunately she'd worn a full cotton skirt. She settled down on the floor, cross-legged, and leaned against the wall. Nurse Sylvère continued to watch her with an expression of grim concentration.

Casually, as if she were accustomed to sitting on the floor in public places, Rosie took out the day's *Le Monde* from her string bag and found an article she'd been reading. In five minutes she would return to the desk and ask to use the telephone. At least she could leave messages for the doctors who had seen Serge.

She must not doze off. If she fell asleep, Serge might disappear. She tried to imagine shopping for dinner as if he would join her, then standing in the kitchen peeling vegetables. In time he would come. Potatoes, there had to be potatoes. You could believe in potatoes. While waiting, she would turn on a lamp.

When the elevator door opened Rosie moved to rise, but no one came out. In several seconds the doors shut automatically. She put the newspaper aside. Hélène Sylvère was now preoccupied with a chart. Rosie closed her eyes, reminding herself that she could cry later, back in the apartment. She had to stay in control for Serge's sake.

"Rosie?" a familiar voice called.

She opened her eyes and saw Thierry walking towards her.

"Why are you sitting there?" he asked.

She stood up as he reached to embrace her.

"She wouldn't let me see Serge — that horrible nurse." The force of Thierry's embrace comforted Rosie. "She's out of some horror movie. Where is he? What's happened?"

"He's in a coma," Thierry said.

"What's going on? They're killing him."

Thierry held on to Rosie's shoulders. "He may not make it."

"That's impossible. Did you see him?"

"I've been with him all evening. But he can't talk. I don't think he knew I was there."

"Why's he getting worse? Why aren't they doing something?"

"I only know what the doctor told me . . ."

"Which one? Chollet or . . ."

"They've all seen him today. His liver's failing."

"Can't they operate?"

"They drained some fluid from his stomach — it was causing the bloating."

"When?"

"This afternoon. I was there. They gave him a local anaesthetic and then . . ."

Rosie looked away. "I have to see him. Is he in pain?"

"Not in a coma. I don't think he feels anything now."

"But he'll pull through, he'll . . ."

"The doctors don't know . . ."

"Don't say that. I want to see him right now."

With Hélène Sylvère watching them, Thierry put his arm around Rosie and led her down the corridor. She avoided his eyes deliberately. "This way," he said, as they entered a large room where pale yellow curtains separated four beds. Without speaking, Rosie turned to him. "Over there," he whispered.

She hurried to the farthest bed and pushed the curtain aside. Serge seemed perfectly still, like one of the carved stone figures that lie so peacefully on medieval crypts. She stepped close to the bed and leaned over, kissing him lightly at the corner of his mouth. Then she kissed him again.

Thierry stood at the foot of the bed, his face dark with grief.

"I'm here now," Rosie said, listening for Serge's breathing. "I'm sorry I'm late, but I'm here now." She reached for his hand. "All these tubes. Once you start getting better they'll take them out."

A nurse joined Thierry, and Rosie turned for an instant to see her face. Then they stepped back and spoke softly in words that she couldn't hear.

Serge appeared to be breathing evenly.

"I won't be late again," Rosie said. "And tomorrow's Saturday, I'll see you first thing in the morning."

As Thierry joined her Rosie saw that the nurse wanted them to leave. She nodded, squeezing Serge's hand. It felt warm but lifeless. "Till the morning," she said.

There was no change in Serge's breathing, or in his expression, but Rosie felt certain that he knew she was with him.

Back in the corridor, she covered her face with her hands, fierce sobs shaking her.

Thierry reached for her shoulder but Rosie pulled away, and without a sound began walking toward the elevator. Following, he allowed her to keep a lead. At the elevator she pushed the button, and then said, "None of you believe in Serge."

Thierry didn't reply. The elevator made rumbling sounds as it approached their floor.

"I'm sorry. Okay? But I'm going out of my mind."

"Why don't you spend the night with Renée and me? I think it might be a good idea."

"No. I need to sleep in my own bed." The words sounded more abrupt than she'd intended.

"You could phone Odile from our place. They have to know."

"I can't talk to her tonight, Thierry. Would you mind phoning for me? You know them better anyway."

"Of course not."

"I'm sorry, I just want to be by myself."

"You don't have to be."

Rosie smiled. "I know that. Thanks. Just ride home with me on the subway. That'll help."

Somehow Rosie got home and into bed. A dead light filled the window but she couldn't be bothered to close the drapes. To her surprise she fell into a deep, exhausting, dreamless sleep. She awoke the next morning, shortly after nine o'clock, to a ringing telephone. An anonymous low voice from the hospital explained that Monsieur Serge Deneau had died in the night and asked if she would please make the suitable arrangements.

13

*W*HERE DO YOU THINK he should be buried?" Odile asked, declining Rosie's offer of coffee a second time.

Mme Deneau had not accompanied her daughter to Rosie's apartment, deciding instead to remain behind in the flat of an old family friend, Jean Berthelot, with whom she and Odile were staying. The friend, a man in his mid-seventies, had come with Odile. He sat beside her on the sofa while Rosie wondered what kind of protection he offered.

"Do you have a preference?" Odile asked. She wore a black silk dress with an irregular pattern of small patches of white and pale pink. It wasn't the kind of dress Rosie would wear, too gracious-lady for her, but she admired it. Odile had prepared to enter the lion's den by becoming the beast.

"In Paris, I think. Serge loved Paris."

"Maman would prefer to have him buried in the family plot."

Rosie hadn't expected this. "But that's in the country, isn't it?"

"I was very fond of Serge," Jean Berthelot said as Rosie refilled his mug.

"Yes," Odile replied, watching him. She continued, "Serge knew that Maman wants all of us to be buried in the family plot."

"He never mentioned that to me."

"No, I suppose he wasn't planning on dying."

Rosie wanted to dump the pot of hot coffee in her well-composed lap. She knew that Odile could be outrageous — after all, she'd slept with her own stepfather — but had rarely seen her in action.

"I'd much rather he be buried in Paris. I'm sure that's what he'd want. He lived here most of his life."

Odile ignored the objection. "I'm afraid you're overruled."

"Then why did you ask? If it's only rhetorical."

"It's democratic," Odile corrected. "I agree with my mother. And we've already paid for the funeral."

"That isn't necessary."

"We can bury our own," Odile said.

"They've already paid for the funeral," Jean Berthelot repeated. The idea seemed to please him, for he smiled broadly.

Exasperated, Rosie put down the coffee pot and returned to her chair.

"There are several things we need from you," Odile continued. "You'll have to make a selection of clothes for Serge . . ."

"I've already thought of that."

"A suit, a shirt, and a tie, that's all, and take them to the undertaker. I've written the address on a card for you."

"What about shoes and . . ."

"Unnecessary. You only need to take the items I've listed. They're written on the back of the card."

"I picked out his brown corduroy suit." Rosie paused. "It was his favorite. And a shirt and tie I bought him the last time I went home, to Pittsburgh."

"Pittsburgh," Jean Berthelot repeated, with curiosity.

"Yes, Jean, Pittsburgh," Odile said.

"Where is that?" he asked.

"Not now, please," Odile said.

Rosie thought that Jean Berthelot looked at her with a sympathetic eye.

"Of course the funeral will be private."

"That isn't fair," Rosie exclaimed. "Serge has many friends."

"Only family at the funeral," Odile continued. "And you, of course."

"People will want to come to the mortuary chapel. They have a right. Serge would be furious."

"If they come to the mortuary I won't say anything. We'll leave from there on Tuesday morning. I've arranged for a driver — we'll all go in the hearse directly to the cemetery. You're coming, too, Jean."

He nodded, and Rosie thought that she might have an ally. The bully Odile seemed to be enjoying her moment of power.

"Maman doesn't want anyone else coming from the mortuary."

"Then I have no say in the plans," Rosie concluded bitterly.

"They're sensible plans," Odile said.

"I can see that. You've thought of everything."

Rosie had always assumed that Mme Deneau and Odile disapproved of her. Now she wished Serge were here so that she could later say to him, "See, I told you so." She gripped the arm of her chair.

"Everything will be fine," Jean Berthelot said.

Rosie was glad he'd come. Alone, she might have told Odile a thing or two. She might have objected, argued, and been barred from Serge's funeral. Odile, the bully, the snake.

Once they'd gone, Rosie sat in her favorite chair, across from Serge's corner of the sofa, unable to move, numb. She knew that the undertaker was waiting for Serge's suit, but couldn't bring herself to go into the bedroom and pack it, along with the other necessary clothes. Minutes passed, then hours, yet her body refused to leave the chair. She wanted Serge; nothing else. When the telephone rang, she ignored it without wondering who the caller might be. When someone knocked on the door, she ignored that, too. People from school would want to offer condolences, people from the neighborhood would do the same, but she didn't want to listen. If Serge couldn't hear them, why should she?

As the afternoon passed, the telephone rang more frequently. Rosie finally turned down the bell. After selling newspapers Serge always enjoyed visiting the offices of *L'Humanité*, and Rosie often went along. He'd turn in the money and they would have dinner with whoever wanted to join them, and talk about the party, various unions, or the latest political disasters in the news. Every year on May Day Serge had sold lilies of the valley for the newspaper. When, at the end of the day, he would bring home several bouquets, their scent would fill the apartment. "Like a well-kept grave," she'd once teased. No one had the right to demand that Serge's funeral be private.

Occasionally Serge had mentioned visiting Jean Berthelot, who lived not far from the Buttes Chaumont park, but Rosie hadn't met him before. There were so many people Serge knew that she hadn't met. She couldn't recall what he'd said about Berthelot, he spoke of so many people. She should have listened more carefully.

Madame Deneau, Odile: snakes, bullies.

What about Thierry and Renée? They belonged at the funeral. Serge would insist. *Would have.*

Thierry, probably one of the callers.

Rosie forced herself from the chair, then turned up the bell on the telephone. She had to answer it for Serge. The undertaker would want his suit; Nadja, at school, might have heard the news; Renée usually cooked elaborate dinners at the hint of a crisis; Odile still had time to come up with another rule. With luck, she thought, I can stay on the telephone until the funeral.

Three hours later, Rosie's ear hurt from the constant press of the receiver, but the sound of another disembodied voice, any voice, helped to steady her. She began to initiate the calls, recounting Serge's last days, breaking only to make coffee and quickly returning to the phone. She sat with her feet propped up on the old Breton table beside the sofa, her head back, her eyes closed, talking as if her life depended on it. No, she didn't want company; no, she didn't need a thing. And everyone stopped to listen: death could make such demands. She described Dr. Chollet, Dr. Bertin, the nurse from Martinique, Hélène Sylvère and her mole, everyone from the hospital who'd been a part of Serge's dying. She repeated herself, at first without noticing it, and then without caring. She would never tire of repeating it. Other people could reread their holy books for comfort. At moments it seemed that Serge had died so that she could discuss it on the telephone.

The light darkened with night, and still she talked: an old student who'd occasionally come to dinner, more colleagues from school, a neighbor who'd moved to Rouen, they all had a right to hear about Serge. Finally she was so exhausted that she fell asleep on the sofa, but as soon as the room brightened with morning, Rosie showered, dressed, and prepared for the first call of the day.

After leaving Serge's suit with the undertaker, in an office that reminded her of a real estate agent's, where bright samples of small metal tombstone plaques lined one wall, she hurried back to her apartment. Odile, to her surprise, had requested an open coffin. What would people think of that? The body would be on display for viewing — "for goodbyes," as the undertaker had put it — only on Tuesday morning, before it would be driven to the country. "Why not tonight?" Rosie had asked, but he shook his head. "For one hour only, in the morning, until we leave for the cemetery. At the family's request." Rosie had nearly said, "I lived with him, and it's not my request," but his brusque manner flattened her. "Is there a service?" she'd asked, as he stared at her. "No, Madame. None." Obviously Mme Deneau chose the odd time to prevent people from attending, but Rosie knew otherwise. She would spend the day on the telephone, if necessary, exposing the snake.

By Tuesday morning Rosie felt that she had phoned half of Paris. Arriving at the mortuary, which was part of the hospital where Serge had died, she braced herself for Mme Deneau. Nearly a hundred people stood on the sidewalk along rue Belgrand, outside the building, waiting for the doors to open at nine o'clock. Crossing the street to join Thierry and Renée, Rosie noticed several colleagues from school, familiar neighbors she didn't know by name, friends of Serge, people from the newspaper office and the party. Mme Deneau and Odile were nowhere in sight. Rosie felt satisfied.

Dressed entirely in black, like a widow in one of Lorca's plays, Renée hugged her, saying, "She must be furious."

"They all cared for Serge or they wouldn't have come," Rosie said. Thierry looked as if he'd forgotten to shave, which surprised her. "Are they inside?" she asked.

"They went in a while ago, through the side entrance. I don't think they saw us."

"I don't want to talk to anyone yet," Rosie said.

The crowd began to move toward the door that had finally been opened. Rosie and the Roussels kept to the rear, near the curb. When anyone caught her eye she nodded, but looked quickly away.

"Are you sure you won't come to the cemetery?" Rosie asked.

Thierry looked down at the sidewalk while Renée said, "It's not worth an argument with them. Serge would hate that."

Serge had disliked any kind of personal confrontation, although Rosie didn't want to be reminded of it.

"She's a witch," Rosie said. "I have some rights too."

"We'll just go inside for a while," Thierry said.

They were closer to the door now, and Rosie could see that they would have to wait for people to leave the room where Serge's coffin must have been placed.

"Do you know all these people?" Renée asked.

"Not everyone," Rosie said with a smile. "People loved Serge, you see?"

Renée put an arm around her shoulders. "You'll be all right," she said firmly.

"I don't know. I'm not sure I want to be all right."

Thierry cleared his throat.

"Why did he have to die?" Rosie asked. "It isn't fair."

No one answered. She took a Kleenex from her purse and wiped her eyes. They stood in the same spot for almost ten minutes. Gradually the crowd moved again.

"I don't want to ride in the same car as Odile," Rosie said.

"You don't have a choice," Thierry replied.

"I'll do it for Serge."

It was a bright early September day, clear as glass, and the sun warmed their heads.

"We'll never leave here by ten o'clock," Rosie said, looking at her watch.

Renée looked at her own watch. "It doesn't matter," she said.

"No. We don't have to punch a time clock." The idea struck Rosie as funny and she smiled.

In another ten minutes they had entered the small mortuary chapel, and Rosie could see Serge's coffin at the end of an aisle. Folding chairs had been set up in rows, as if a meeting were about to begin.

"Even in the hospital we never talked about death," Rosie said.

"Never?" Renée asked.

Rosie appeared not to hear. The spray of roses she had ordered stood at the foot of the coffin, blazing red. Mme Deneau and Odile were seated in the first row of chairs, near the wall, with Jean Berthelot.

As she stepped toward the coffin Rosie looked into Serge's face. He almost resembled himself.

She stood unable to move in any direction and Thierry came forward at once, reaching for her elbow.

"He would hate this," she said. "He hated open coffins."

Thierry held her by the arm.

"At my father's funeral it was closed," she added.

"Do you want to sit down?" he asked.

"I don't know what I want." She pulled away from him and rested her hand on Serge's. "We never talked about death," she repeated.

"Do you want to stay here by yourself?" Thierry asked.

"No," Rosie sighed, turning away from the coffin. Mme Deneau, she saw, had been watching her. The funeral director now stood beside her chair.

Rosie went to greet Mme Deneau, who remained seated.

"We'll close the coffin once everyone leaves the room," the undertaker explained. A tall, slender man in his sixties, he had large, slablike hands. Had they touched Serge's body?

Jean Berthelot stood immediately, and Odile joined him. She again wore the black dress with pastel splotches. "It's almost 10:30," Odile remarked. "Are you ready to leave?"

"Yes," Rosie deferred. Mme Deneau, her face heavily powdered, had on a deep purple suit trimmed in black along the cuffs and lapels.

"Then we can go out to the hearse."

Rosie wished that she'd taken time to find something other than a white blouse and black pleated skirt. Like an aging schoolgirl, she thought. Except that schoolgirls no longer dressed that way. Over one arm she carried an unnecessary navy blue raincoat.

Following Jean Berthelot, Rosie looked back at the coffin a final time. The undertaker and his assistant blocked her view.

The ride to the cemetery would take at least two hours, she calculated as the hearse pulled into traffic. Fortunately Rosie sat in the back seat, alone, behind the Deneaus and their friend. She looked out the window as they left Paris behind, vaguely listening to the amiable conversation going on without her. Jean Berthelot was describing his grandchildren — a remarkable lot, he believed — and then the driver joined in, offering his own anecdotes. Mme Deneau, without grandchildren, had several theories on how to raise them. Children today were all the same: ungrateful, selfish, spoiled, trouble. A strong hand was needed.

Paris gave way to its suburbs, then a bleak industrial wasteland, and, finally, a hint of the coming countryside.

Schools today were to blame, Odile was insisting. What did teachers know?

Childless Odile. Rosie grimaced. Sitting there, next to her mother, who had loved the same man. Rosie couldn't begin to imagine what her life had been like. She had no spare compassion this morning.

And then she heard talk of stopping for lunch. After all, they'd had a late start, and the driver was hungry. In the next village was a good small restaurant, family-run. Everyone would welcome a proper lunch.

Rosie searched in her purse for another Kleenex, then wiped her eyes, glad to be ignored. *Serge: why did you leave me?*

As the hearse drew to a halt outside an old house, Odile turned to Rosie and announced, over the top of her seat, that they were stopping for lunch. "I'm hungry, too," Rosie said, even though she wasn't.

The empty, dark restaurant consisted of a small main room with half a dozen tables overlooking a patio, which had not been set up for guests. A heavy oak sideboard displayed several desserts, and on the opposite wall hung a large watercolor of the restaurant's garden in a style evoking Monet. Mme Deneau pointed to the table of her choice and everyone followed.

Rosie contrived to sit between Jean Berthelot and the driver, whom she saw up close for the first time. A man in his late fifties, in a dark uniform, he seemed inappropriately cheerful. Perhaps it was the thought of a free meal, for Odile had insisted that everyone be her guest.

The proprietor arrived at their table and recited the routine menu for a three-course meal. Rosie listened as Jean Berthelot and the driver debated the merits of escargots and smoked mackerel. Distracted, Odile seemed to be eyeing the array of sweets on the sideboard. No one mentioned wine.

Rabbit with prunes, roast pork loin, *sole bonne femme,* Rosie heard the choice of main courses repeated another time. She ordered the sole, eager to be finished with lunch. Serge had never belonged to these people.

They ate in silence, except for Berthelot, who remarked on each course. The leeks vinaigrette were to be recommended. Rosie feared she would scream. Then he turned to her and asked if she liked teaching.

"Yes," Rosie mumbled, swallowing a piece of bread.

"I've always admired teachers," he said. "It must be difficult work. My daughter's a teacher."

She began to choke, and covered her mouth with her hand.

"Is something wrong?" he asked.

She shook her head, choking harder.

"Perhaps a fish bone?"

Odile was staring at her angrily.

Rosie shook her head again.

The driver called for a glass of water as tears filled her eyes.

Oh God, Serge.

The water appeared and Rosie took a gulp, then a second one.

"Breathe deeply," suggested the driver.

Mme Deneau had set down her fork to watch.

"I'm sorry," Rosie apologized. The room was absurdly hot.

"Down the wrong pipe," Jean Berthelot observed.

Rosie couldn't stop herself from laughing, and he joined her immediately. "I guess so," she said.

"Now finish your fish," he said.

"Thank you, no, I've had enough."

Odile and Mme Deneau had returned to their plates, and silence claimed the table. Rosie wondered if she had the courage to survive dessert.

By the time they reseated themselves in the hearse, Jean Berthelot and Rosie spoke like old friends. Odile frequently looked at her mother, who appeared not to notice. Mme Deneau had a wistful expression that troubled Rosie. For the first time she could see Serge in his mother's face.

The silence of lunch continued as they drove. Rosie closed her eyes and leaned her head back on the leather seat until the hearse began to slow down at the edge of Mme Deneau's village.

Surrounded by an old black iron fence, the treeless cemetery looked almost stern to her. Why shouldn't death be as hard as stone? it seemed to warn. No wonder that Serge never brought her here when they'd visited. A small group of people had already gathered at the gate. Several of the men, Rosie guessed, would be pallbearers. She recognized no one.

The driver motioned to two men to join him, and they hoisted the coffin out of the back of the hearse. Mme Deneau and Odile followed them.

Above, a wide blue sky, with barely a cloud, graced the afternoon. Abutting the back of the cemetery, a screen of tall poplars shielded the view of distant rolling hills. There were vineyards somewhere beyond the poplars, Rosie recalled Serge once telling her: a postcard vision of the French countryside. This place had nothing to do with Serge.

Jean Berthelot took Rosie's arm, steadying himself as they walked through the tombstones toward a marble obelisk, its base covered with a dozen bronze markers bearing the names of various members of Serge's family. Nearby Rosie saw a freshly dug grave, earth piled alongside it.

"Odile hadn't planned on stopping for lunch," Berthelot whispered. "But the driver insisted."

14

THERE'S A SHORTAGE OF wood, and coffins are now made of cardboard. The churches are full of dead bodies. They line the aisles, waiting.

A woman stands at the cathedral doors again, then goes inside.

Lights only from candles, when anyone can find them, and matches, rarer now.

When one of the priests — the young one — leaves the cathedral, she watches for the other while scanning bodies for anything that might prove useful. They're all wrapped in sheets so it's hard to guess which are worth a closer look. Some almost new socks stick out from one and she bends to pull them off quickly. Hard, slender feet like wood. She stuffs the socks in her pocket and moves on to the next body — an old woman, she can tell, because an arm has slipped out of the sheet and there's a label on it. Most of the bodies are either very young or very old.

Suddenly she sees that a child of perhaps five or six — it's hard to tell — is following her.

The children have rickets. She's watched their stomachs bloat full of emptiness, fleshy balloons.

What is it to be human anymore, she sometimes wonders. Then: so your stomach's empty, well join me, come sleep in my cellar. A rubbish heap — like those on the street corners, like all of us — but come sleep in my cellar.

"Your parents?" she asks the child, "Where are your parents?"

He looks up at her blankly.

"Do you live nearby? Are you lost?"

No answer. Then he takes the hem of her coat in his hand.

"What's your name?" she asks, wishing he'd go away, not look at her, not search her face. "What do you want?"

And she knows, as sure as if he'd spoken, that he has chosen her in the same way one kitten from a litter picks its mistress.

"Let's go," she tells him, but he only holds fast.

Outside the cathedral men retch against a wall.

Nothing else to do, she takes the child home with her. He never makes a sound, never cries. There's little to feed him but raw beets. She tries but he can't swallow, his tongue is white and rough.

The child sleeps in a corner of the cellar, and she watches him. His body is covered with sores. She stares at them, decides, and puts her hands around his neck — thin, small — pressing her thumbs into the throat. Pressing harder. The child barely wakes, struggles. I'm trying to die, she thinks. And I'm helping you.

"Mama!" shouted Rosie, waking. She reached for her bedside lamp, turned it on and sat trembling.

Not quite five AM, she read the clock's face, thinking, I can't stand this anymore.

She looked at Serge's empty half of the bed, caressed it, and then got up and went into the living room. She stared at the telephone. Nobody wanted a call before dawn.

Back in the bedroom, Rosie dressed and combed her

hair, ignoring the strands clinging to the comb. It would be almost midnight in New York. She could phone Deb instead of answering her letter. But then she'd have to tell her about Serge. Impossible.

Serge had been buried only five days before, but already the funeral seemed an unreal memory from a long-gone past. This grieved Rosie, who found it somehow disloyal. But the details evaded her. She could only remember tossing a handful of dry earth into the grave while no one said a word, and then Odile announced "It's over." Mme Deneau had invited some of the villagers back to the house, but she'd told Rosie and Jean Berthelot to return to Paris with the driver. "I was never part of the family," Rosie had said as they'd settled beside each other in the hearse. "And neither was Serge." She didn't care if he repeated her remark to Odile, although she suspected it would go no further.

In Paris, a letter from Deb was waiting. Rosie put it aside for several days, and finally opened it one morning at breakfast. Deb had won another trip, this time a week in London, but had decided to use only the plane tickets and pick up a flight for Budapest at Heathrow. She felt an ancestral tie to the city — Rosie must too. Wouldn't she join her?

The idea struck Rosie as preposterous. She would say that it was impossible to take time off from work. Poor Deb, with no life but her contests and her groups and classes. And now, Rosie thought, I'm alone, just like her.

Rosie had spent the days since the funeral talking about Serge to anyone who would listen. She'd already visited Jean Berthelot, had dinner with Renée and Thierry, and also with several friends from school. Now her first weekend without Serge stared her down. There was no hospital to visit, and she would never see Serge again. Renée had offered to drop by while Rosie packed up his clothes, but she wasn't ready for that.

She tried to see his grave in her mind. Why couldn't she remember? She kept imagining Deb beside her, but that was at their father's funeral. At her mother's, she'd stood between him and Deb. Uncle Aladar had arranged for that funeral, and money must have changed hands, since there was no mention of Elza's overdose. "The accident," everyone called it. As usual Uncle Aladar had known how to take care of things. But it had probably been Aunt Pearl who'd ordered the mounds of deli food — pastrami and cole slaw. She could still see the dining room table set up with her mother's best china. Of course some Orthodox cousins had refused to touch the food because the Kamin household wasn't kosher — she hadn't thought of that in years. Relatives she barely knew wouldn't touch the food, or use her mother's plates. Rosie closed her eyes to block out the image of people stuffing their mouths. At the inn Mme Deneau had eaten with relish, Odile had chewed so intently that it was audible, even frail old Jean Berthelot had risen to the occasion.

At her mother's grave had she thrown in a handful of earth?

Why did people do that?

Why did Serge have to die?

Shortly before noon there was an unexpected knock on the door. Rosie hurried to it, glad to have company, as Thierry called out his name.

"Maybe I should have phoned first," he apologized. "I hope you don't mind."

"Of course not. I wasn't doing anything special."

"It's chilly out, you can feel winter coming." He wore a heavy sweater of natural-colored wool. "Is there anything you need?"

"Where's Renée?"

"She's meeting with her publisher."

"On Saturday?"

They headed into the living room, toward the sofa, which was piled with the last week's newspapers.

"She says writers never stop working."

"Forgive my mess," Rosie said, gesturing at several plates of half-eaten food on the coffee table. "I keep meaning to clean up." She tossed the newspapers on the floor.

"How are you doing?" he asked.

She shrugged. "Do you want a sandwich? Or something?"

"No, thanks."

"What about you?" she asked.

"I still can't believe it," he said.

"I know. I keep waiting for Serge to come in the door."

Thierry sat with his elbows on his knees, his hands clasped under his chin.

"You're growing a beard?" she asked.

"I guess so. Why not?"

"What does Renée think?"

"She hasn't said."

"Really? Remember when Serge had a moustache?"

He nodded. "That was a while ago."

"I liked him better without it."

"You know, I talked to him almost every day for the past thirty years."

She was grateful to have a friend like Thierry, who had cared for Serge. "You should have something of Serge's, some kind of memento. Maybe his watch? At the hospital they gave me an envelope filled with his things — his wallet, all that — and the other night I finally opened it. Other people's things always seem so fragile. Does that sound silly?"

"Not to me."

"The watch is a good one. I want you to have it."

She moved to stand up but Thierry stopped her. "Not now," he said.

"You know I always thought we'd grow old together, the way you and Renée will."

"Don't say that."

"But it's true."

"Renée and I, we don't have much of a marriage."

Rosie didn't speak immediately. "What do you mean?"

"Serge never told you? He promised he wouldn't. You know he had no patience with gossips."

"What didn't he tell me?"

"About me and Renée."

Rosie leaned forward.

"We haven't slept together in years."

She felt the air around her had suddenly thinned.

"Five years, actually."

"That's awful," Rosie said. "Is there someone else?"

"No. At least I don't think so. But what's worse, I don't even care."

"What did Serge say?"

"He never gave advice, he just listened. He knew that people never take advice anyway. They only want you to confirm what they're going to do."

"I don't know what to say."

"Maybe I shouldn't be telling you this. I'm glad Serge kept it to himself."

Rosie wouldn't admit it to Thierry, but she felt hurt that Serge had kept his secret. "Yet you've stayed together," she said.

"If you can call it that. We share an apartment, that's more like it."

"I never guessed," Rosie said.

"We didn't want you to."

She looked puzzled.

"Not just you. Everyone, I mean. Renée thinks there's nothing wrong with the way we're living. It suits her."

"But not you?"

He didn't reply, perhaps from embarrassment, and Rosie wished that he hadn't made the confession. She reached for a small sofa pillow and put her arms around it.

"Let's talk about something else," he said.

Rosie ran a finger around the seam at the edge of the pillow.

"You'll stay in this apartment? People say you shouldn't make changes too quickly. After someone dies."

"Before you came I was trying to remember my mother's funeral. And my father's, too. I guess I'm just not very good at remembering funerals. Deb knows every detail. She thrives on details like that."

Thierry smiled. "It fits," he said.

"She's just won another trip, and she wants me to meet her. In Budapest."

"Why don't you go? Serge would tell you to."

"Probably. But what would I do in Budapest?"

"Renée was there once," he said. "You should ask her about it."

"Do you hate her?" Rosie asked.

"No. It's not her fault. No one's to blame."

"I never really trusted her."

"That's not fair," he said defensively.

"Yes it is. And you know what, I don't think she likes me very much."

Thierry didn't answer.

"I'm right, aren't I?"

"The two of you were never close," he agreed.

"That's an evasion." She saw there was no way to make him understand.

He sighed. "What's the use? With Serge dead, things won't be the same."

"We can still be friends," she said, her voice rising. "You're still my friend, aren't you?"

"Of course I am."

"Then what do you mean?"

"Maybe this sounds crazy, but somehow when I could talk to Serge about things it made them easier."

"That's how I felt about him too. Look, do you want some wine? There's a bottle of plonk in the kitchen."

"Why not?"

"When I got back from the funeral I tried to get drunk, I couldn't sleep and I couldn't stop crying so I finished half a bottle of wine, some awful stuff, but it just made me sick."

Rosie went into the kitchen, found two glasses, the wine, and a corkscrew. She must remember to wash the dishes, later. What else hadn't Serge told her?

"I keep having the same dream," she said, returning to the sofa as Thierry reached for the corkscrew.

"What about?"

She described her cathedral dream with a shudder. "What do you think it means?"

"I'm not good with dreams," he said. "Renée's the one."

They looked at each other and burst out laughing.

"Who knows? Maybe by telling it to you I've broken the pattern."

"I don't think you can jinx a dream."

"Don't say that. Please. This one needs jinxing."

"Have you heard from Benyoub?"

"That's another strange thing. He came to the hospital several times but I haven't heard from him since . . ." she paused.

Thierry poured the wine and handed her a glass.

"He seems to have vanished," she added. "Did Serge talk about him with you?"

"He felt sorry for him. And I think he rather liked him, too. That's about all."

"You're sure?"

He nodded. "There's not much to tell. Serge had a cousin who was killed in the Algerian war. But that has nothing to do with Benyoub."

"As long as you're telling me the truth."

"I am, now, but I did lie to you before."

Rosie looked at the wine glass in her hand. How often she and Serge had sat like this, drinking and talking.

"In the hospital, when I mentioned Serge's doctor . . ."

"Which one?" she interrupted.

"Chollet, I think."

"They were all awful."

"I didn't tell you exactly what he said."

"Yes?"

"He thought that if Serge pulled through he'd only have a year or two to live. A year or two, that's what he said. But Serge didn't want you to know. Not then."

"He knew?"

"Yes."

"Why tell me now?"

"I don't want any lies between us. And maybe you should know."

"Is that everything?"

He shook his head. "The night we took him to the hospital, when he was bleeding . . ."

"That wasn't the first time?" she asked.

Thierry looked at her with embarrassment. "Before he went into the hospital in July he'd thrown up blood. They wanted to do a liver biopsy but couldn't, not when someone's still bleeding. So that's why he was going back for more tests. It was really for the biopsy. They'd only taken x-rays the first time."

"And no one thought to tell me?"

"Serge didn't want to frighten you."

"As if I were a child."

"He loved you so much, he hated to see you frightened."

Rosie put down her glass. If only he would go.

In the following days invitations piled on top of each other, and Rosie accepted them, as long as people would listen while she spoke of Serge. And each time that she described the funeral, and Mme Deneau or Odile, she saw it from a new angle. "It's hard to associate an unfamiliar cemetery with someone you love," she said one evening to colleagues from Continental, over dinner. If nobody much cared about her observations, Rosie didn't notice. They mattered to her. And everyone kept phoning. Everyone but Benyoub.

She began to wish he would call, and wanted to apologize for shouting at him in the restaurant. Perhaps he'd never returned to the hospital; perhaps he didn't even know that Serge had died. Certainly he'd want to know. She had to tell him about Serge.

On the Sunday afternoon after her visit with Thierry she went to find Benyoub. Hadn't Thierry assured her that Serge had liked Ben? Serge, a good judge of character.

Rosie hoped she would recognize the building as she turned onto Benyoub's street, crowded with a moving wave of people that frightened her. This time she hadn't worn any jewelry, and she carried less money than usual in her wallet, just in case. Here, she thought, approaching a building with half a dozen North African children playing on the steps. A small girl of four or five rocked a doll in her arms.

Excusing herself, Rosie mounted the steps. The dark, dirty corridors would be the same in all of these buildings, yet she felt certain that she recognized this one. Surely the young woman who had closed the door on her knew Benyoub's name. Today she would refuse to leave until she found out where he lived.

As soon as she knocked on the door someone called out, but Rosie didn't understand the words. Then the door opened, and Hamed Benali stood before her. "Rosie Kamin?" he said, his eyes widening.

Rosie swallowed uncomfortably.

"It's been fifteen years. At least," he said.

She looked into his face. He smiled at her with curiosity.

"At least," she repeated.

"But come in. You're welcome in my home. How did you know where to find me?"

His body had thickened, become stocky and powerful. She remembered the musky scent of his skin: he'd always claimed that Europeans bathed too frequently. Benyoub had retained a hint of his youth, of the beautiful boy, but Hamed had been transformed into his own father. Today he wore a crisply ironed white shirt, open at the neck, as Ben had. Perhaps they used the same laundry.

"Actually, I'm looking for Benyoub."

"My cousin Benyoub?"

So he could still play his old games. "Yes, your cousin," she said.

"Come inside, please," he motioned, stepping away from the doorway.

She entered, wishing she hadn't come.

"Benyoub isn't here now," he said. The wrinkles on his forehead deepened as he spoke. "Perhaps I can help you."

"I wanted to see Ben."

"Ah," Hamed smiled. "Has he been borrowing money again?"

Rosie bristled, and hoped he wouldn't notice. "No," she replied.

The living room was poorly lit. Its walls had been pa-
pered with *toile de jute,* a dark brown burlap covering.

"He was kind to . . ." she stopped, wondering if Ben had
mentioned Serge to him. Hamed was the first person she
didn't want to tell about Serge.

"Please, sit down. This is most unexpected."

"Yes," she agreed.

All these years he had gone on living his life. Yet he didn't
appear to be weighed down by it, as she might have pre-
dicted. His eyes were bright, clear. Suddenly Rosie realized
that Hamed wasn't smoking. She'd rarely seen him without
a cigarette in his hand.

"You're not smoking?" she asked.

"I gave it up years ago," he said. A smile flickered on his
lips. That old smile. The look from on high.

Noises rose up from the street and managed to penetrate
the living room, though the large windows were draped
with a heavy material almost as dark as the walls.

"You've been here before?" he asked.

"Several months ago."

He folded his hands as he listened.

"In the summer. A young girl came to the door, she had
a veil . . ."

"Djellaba," he corrected. "That must have been Malika.
She told me a woman had come looking for my cousin."

Why did he keep calling Benyoub his cousin? "I don't
know," she said. "Is she your wife?"

Hamed grinned. "No," he said.

"I wasn't sure if she understood me," Rosie added. "But
I thought she recognized Benyoub's name."

"She did. Benyoub is her father."

For a moment Rosie couldn't breathe. "I see."

Hamed crossed his legs, clearly amused by her surprise.
"And you," he said, "do you not have children? You know

they say that twelve children is the greatest blessing from Allah."

Rosie shook her head. How could he ask her that? Hamed, of all men.

"You've refused your destiny," he said.

"Forget it, Hamed. Are you living back in the fifteenth century? I read that the birthrate in Algeria increases three per cent a year. Think what that means."

"My people . . ."

She wouldn't listen. Their baby would have been about the same age as the young girl, Malika.

"Does he live here, then?"

"No. But Malika stays with us. With my family."

She wanted to hear more about Malika but wouldn't give him the satisfaction of asking. Was Hamed telling the truth? He'd always lied naturally, expansively. "I thought you were living in Algeria again."

"Who told you that?" He paused, and before she could reply, said, "Ah, Ben. I have a place there too."

Sure, Rosie thought. And I just bought Versailles. "Do you have an address for him?"

"Only a telephone number," Hamed said.

"Has he gone back to Algeria?"

"No. Why do you think that?"

"When you see him next will you ask him to phone me?"

"You're in such a hurry," he observed.

"I don't mean to be rude," she apologized.

"You were never rude."

"I need to talk with him. About a mutual friend. May I have his number?"

"Ben used to say that you had all the luck. I'll get some paper."

Hamed left the room and Rosie looked about. On every available surface stood Algerian pottery and metal bowls, as if somebody had raided a souk. Scattered over the floor, old patterned rugs gave the shabby room an air of faded luxury. There wasn't a book in sight, which puzzled Rosie — Hamed had always been reading something thick and obscure. He'd once thrown a book at her when she told him not to study so much. In the youth hostel where they'd met, he had lent her a book; they'd both loved youth hostels.

"My wife and children went out for the afternoon," Hamed explained as he returned, handing Rosie a piece of paper with a telephone number written across it. In his other hand he carried a plate of dried dates. "Are you still teaching?"

"Yes," she said, standing.

"And you must go at once?"

"Yes."

"But something's wrong. That's why you're here, isn't it?"

"My husband died," she blurted out. "Ben visited him in the hospital. I thought he'd want to know."

"I'm sorry," Hamed said. He seemed unable to decide whether to return to his chair or continue standing with the plate in his hand. "Life can be difficult."

Her eyes were brimming with tears and she saw him reach out toward her.

"Truly I'm sorry," he said.

"Would you ask Ben to call me?"

"Of course," he said flatly.

She watched him draw back, perhaps offended by her refusal of comfort.

Weepy, pathetic fool! She hated herself. She thought of begging his forgiveness.

"Be careful of Benyoub," he said.

For a moment she was afraid that Hamed was about to grab her by the wrist. "I can take care of myself," she muttered.

"With the aid of Allah."

The hostility she felt now overwhelmed her, as if Hamed were responsible for Serge's death. For every failure in her life. Absurd, she knew, but felt it just the same.

"You're both lost," he added.

She turned from him and fumbled with the door knob.

"You and Benyoub."

Hamed was always posturing. She had to get away from him.

"The door's locked," he said. "You have to unlock it first."

His arm came toward her again and she nearly cried out.

"There. I don't want to keep you here."

He seemed to be growing taller in front of her.

"I never invited you here."

As the door came open she pushed past him into the corridor. Weeping, Rosie ran down the stairs. She wasn't sure where she would go, and until she reached the landing, didn't know if Hamed had followed her.

Children were shouting at each other as she stepped into the sunlight, which blinded her. Clutching her purse, she joined the moving crowd, wishing that a taxi would miraculously appear.

How dare he speak to her like that! She'd meant no harm.

She wiped her eyes with the back of her hand.

You're both lost.

She wanted to be dead, with Serge.

Back in her apartment she undressed and climbed into bed. At least she could hide there until morning. She would force her mind to go blank; why remember her pain? If only she could will herself beside Serge, in Mme Deneau's glistening new coffin. No one need know.

Shortly after midnight the telephone rang. People never called then — it must be Benyoub. Rosie answered it eagerly.

"It's me. Deb." Pause. "Your sister."

"Deb? Is something wrong? Where are you?"

"In New York. Where else would I be? What time is it there?"

"Midnight," Rosie said.

"I'm really excited about this trip, Rosie. I hadn't won anything for months — I needed a win. I hope you're coming."

Rosie didn't reply.

"You're coming, aren't you?"

"Serge died."

"What did you say?"

"Serge died. A week ago."

"No," Deb said slowly.

"I wouldn't make that up."

"What happened?"

Rosie explained about the coma, the hospital, the intensive care ward.

"But what did he actually die of?" Deb asked.

"A combination of things. I can't talk about it."

"It's terrible," Deb offered. "I'm sorry."

Rosie wished that she could see the expression on Deb's face.

"Serge was always nice to me."

"Everyone loved Serge," Rosie said.

"Listen, I don't mean to cut this short, but you can tell me all about it in Budapest."

"I don't know."

"Now you have to come. I won't take no for an answer."

"What about your friend Helen? I thought she went along on your trips."

"Not any more. She told everyone at work that I'm obsessed with contests, that I'm like an alcoholic. But it's not true. They're just a hobby."

"Of course," Rosie said reassuringly, hating the word "alcoholic."

"No one talks about the dark side of winning contests. I could probably write a book, but this call's costing a fortune; I won't go into it now."

Rosie remembered Deb sitting beside their mother at the kitchen table, pasting green savings stamps into a book. Deb's favorite job around the house. Had it started her on the road to contests? "Don't lick the stamps, use a wet sponge or you'll be sick from the glue," Elza always cautioned.

"You'll meet me, won't you?"

"I may not be much company," Rosie said.

"It'll be good for you to get away."

"Maybe," Rosie said.

"Then that's settled."

"If I can get the time off. I'll have to ask."

"Don't take any shit from them. They'll understand you have to get away. What with Serge dying, I mean. I'm sure he'd tell you to come. Last week I phoned cousin Joel and got him to find Mama's address in Budapest."

Cousin Joel, Rosie thought. What was this cousin bit? It made him sound like a Jewish hillbilly. *Go on, be critical,* Serge would have said. *You only hurt yourself.*

"You know how Uncle Aladar saved everything. It was on some old letters . . ."

Budapest, Rosie sighed.

". . . and I want to see the building."

"I never thought of that."

"You have to keep going," Deb said intensely. "That's all you can do."

Was that meant to be comforting? Rosie wondered. People seemed to like saying it.

15

*A*FTER SEVERAL GLOOMY days sunlight finally broke through Budapest's gray, polluted air to beat on the side of the redbrick synagogue. Across the sooty plaza stood Rosie and Deb, trenchcoats draped over their shoulders. Pigeons surrounded them, some sleeping brazenly at the base of the temple's arches, and as Rosie shielded her eyes from the sun with her right hand she muttered, "I hate those nasty birds." The Dohány Street synagogue was the largest in Europe, though not the oldest.

Deb ignored her sister's remark and continued flipping through the pages of a guidebook. "Listen," she announced. "Designed between 1854 and 1859 in a Romantic style with Byzantine-Moorish elements . . ."

Rosie thought of someone reading off the ingredients on a tin can. "But you aren't really sure that Mama ever came here," she said.

"I know." Deb sighed. "If only Uncle Aladar didn't have Alzheimer's. There's a lot of things I'd like to ask him."

"Have you tried? I thought that memory of recent events went first."

"He doesn't even know what planet he's on," Deb said impatiently, holding up the book. "Do you want to hear this or not?"

"No," Rosie answered. "Can't we just go inside?"

For Deb it was synagogues, for Serge it had been cathedrals, and Rosie felt that she'd only traded one kind of temple for another. Serge had meticulously organized their vacations to Mortagne-sur-Sèvre and Briançon and Saint-Emilion, as if planning a crucial campaign; Rosie had only to pack her own suitcase, aware that perfection awaited them.

"Oh, shit!" exclaimed Deb, reading again.

"What's wrong?"

"I told you about the Jewish Museum in the synagogue's annex, over there."

"Yes."

"Well it's only open from May 15 to October 15. We've missed it by four days."

"We could double-check with someone," Rosie offered, reaching for the guidebook and consulting the page Deb had been reading.

"We have to do something," Deb said. "I've got to see that museum. I'm not here as a tourist."

Rosie looked at her sister with a mixture of bewilderment and fear. "But if it's closed," she said.

"Come on," Deb said. "I'm going to ask that man."

Heading toward the synagogue, she marched resolutely to an elderly man in a black fedora and a worn black overcoat. He appeared to be reading a bus schedule as he walked.

"Excuse me," she began.

He looked up, smiled and shook his head.

"The museum . . ."

He shook his head again and stared at her.

"Oh, never mind. Thanks."

Rosie joined Deb just as the man hurried past them.

"I'm sure they're all pretending not to speak English," Deb said.

"Can't we just find a place to sit down and have some coffee? We've been walking all morning. I don't think I can take another step."

Deb closed the guidebook and looked about.

"I might collapse right here with all these pigeons."

"You can collapse after we see the cemetery," Deb said. "The guidebook says there's a garden behind the annex that became a cemetery for people from the ghetto killed by the Nazis."

"Sure," Rosie said. "If it gets me closer to a cup of coffee. But you know I hate cemeteries."

"I don't see why," Deb said.

Serge had sometimes called Rosie "*ma petite Juif*," after a song by Maurice Fanon, "La Petite Juif." She didn't want to remember that now. She could hear Deb thinking that he drank himself to death.

"I want to get a few pictures," Deb explained. Around her neck, from a thick leather strap, hung a Japanese camera that she'd recently won, third prize in a contest for a trip to Hawaii. "Okay?"

"You're relentless," Rosie said, shrugging with a laugh. After a few days Deb's behavior was beginning to seem almost normal. "As long as I don't have to be in them."

Wishing that she'd stayed in Paris, Rosie followed Deb like an animal on a short leash. What did Budapest have to do with her? At the Gellért Hotel where they were staying, on the Buda side of the Danube, the sisters shared a room for the first time since they were small children, and Rosie hardly slept for the sound of Deb's snoring, groans, small cries. Deb's notion that she wasn't a tourist but a pilgrim on some romantic adventure no longer amused her, or touched her either. Self-deluded, Deb persisted in believing that a cemetery off a busy street in an old ghetto might change her life. Did she expect to find a revelation there, or would she be satisfied with a few anecdotes that might appeal to her discussion groups?

Certain that she knew too much about cemeteries for another one to matter, Rosie gazed about, trying not to think of Serge's funeral. She saw nothing of interest as Deb bent to look at a gravestone. Her sister could be a remarkably insensitive creature, she'd always known that. If only the dead could haunt you, not just your memories of them.

"I'm finished here," Deb said, joining her again. "What about you?"

"I don't like cemeteries, let's go."

"Didn't you . . ." Deb said, but Rosie cut her off. "I shouldn't have come. I don't want to spoil your vacation; I'm just not up for this."

Now Rosie took the lead and they headed toward the first bench she could spot, next to a concrete planter filled with dried-out earth, cigarette butts, and wads of old Kleenex.

"I thought getting away would be good for you," Deb said as they made themselves comfortable. She set her purse beside her on the bench so that no one would take the empty seat. "What should we do next?"

"I don't know what's wrong with me. I can't think of anything but Serge."

"But he just died," Deb said, putting the guidebook on top of her purse. "That's normal."

"I guess so. And it's not that I want to stop thinking about him. I don't. I just want him to be alive."

Deb looked down at her hands.

"It's all my fault," Rosie said. "I should have seen something was wrong. I mean really wrong. I knew he liked to drink, but he didn't drink that much. Other people drink more and it never bothers them. But the doctors kept implying he was an alcoholic. It's crazy. You don't think he was, do you?"

"People metabolize liquor differently," Deb offered.

"Sure." Rosie sighed bitterly. She reached for her string bag and took out a package of Fig Newtons that Deb had brought from New York. "Do you want one?"

Deb shook her head.

Rosie opened the package and took out two cookies. "I'm ruining your vacation," she said, with mounting apprehension.

Deb didn't reply.

A hundred pigeons had gathered at their feet — black, gray, white, brown, some flecked with green and mauve.

Rosie cringed.

"What's wrong with you?" Deb asked. "They're not going to attack."

Abruptly the birds rose in a mass, the violent sound of their flapping wings making Rosie duck. Half of the flock landed on the window ledges of a nearby building while the others circled in the air and returned to the sidewalk.

"I don't know what I'm supposed to do," Rosie said. Thierry told me the doctors said Serge had only a few years to live, and he knew it all along. But he never told me. Nobody told me a thing."

"Maybe Serge . . ."

"If it was killing him he should have stopped. He should have told me. I could have helped." She bit into a fig bar.

Deb pushed her coat off her shoulders.

"I think he loved me," Rosie said.

"What does love have to do with it?" asked Deb.

"If you love someone you don't have to hide things from them, you can tell them everything. And you know how I hate surprises. Always have. Surprise! Serge is an alcoholic. Surprise! Ben has a teenage daughter."

"What?"

"Yeah, I didn't tell you that. She's fifteen. Malika."

"Fifteen? When did you find out?"

"Before I left."

"Why don't you date Jewish men?" Deb asked suddenly, her voice low and serious. She tilted her head like a caged bird listening to its owner make cooing sounds.

"Oh God," Rosie groaned. "Let's not get into that. Remember our father? You know what he used to write on his letters to me? When he thought he had a point to make? At the top of the page he'd write 'Read this again and again until you understand.'"

"He was a monster," Deb said casually.

"I wouldn't go that far."

"Don't defend him, Rosie."

"I'm not. He was so rigid. If he had an idea about something that's how it was."

"He killed Mama."

Rosie shook her head. "That's not fair."

"I've talked about it with my group. He never understood her. What it meant to be a survivor."

"Why do you say that?"

"We never mentioned it," Deb said. "He was glad to pretend it never happened."

"He ignored everything he didn't like."

"You think that's a virtue?"

"I didn't say that."

"You look like Mama," Deb remarked, "but you're really more like him."

"I said I shouldn't have come."

"I thought maybe we could talk things out. Budapest's neutral ground."

"Neutral ground?" Rosie repeated. "Did somebody in your group say that?"

"Yes, actually."

"This summer, when you came to Paris, did you want to 'talk things out'?"

Deb nodded. "But Paris freaks me. It's so pretty, too pretty. It reminds me of an ornate gutter."

Rosie figured that she would always be the one in the wrong, so the city she lived in had to be wrong too.

"When I got home I told my group about the swastika on your friends' door. 'That's Europe,' they said. 'Nothing ever changes.'"

"Then why did you come back?"

"I thought maybe here, where Mama came from, we could talk. That's why I got her old address from Joel. And then someone in my group recognized it. His parents lived there too: 13 Király utca. It's not far from here. That's why I think this could have been their synagogue. They weren't Orthodox, and the other synagogues around here are."

"I know all of this means something to you, but I don't understand."

"We don't always have to be the same," Deb said. "Two sisters who can't talk. You're almost Mama's age when she killed herself."

"I'm only forty," Rosie said.

"She was forty-five."

Rosie brushed a strand of hair from her face. "Do we have to talk about it?"

"She killed herself," Deb repeated. "She killed herself. Think of what she carried around inside of her."

"Don't, please."

"With no one to listen."

"Please."

"In two years I'll be forty. And then forty-five, like she was."

Tears filled Rosie's eyes.

"I'm not going to run away from it," Deb said. "I won't be like Daddy. It's better to cry."

"Mama killed him too," Rosie said flatly. "By what she did."

"Everyone in our house was dead. Don't you see? All of us. We were all dead."

"Why are you doing this?" Rosie asked.

"Because it's about time we admitted it."

"And then?"

"I don't know. I have to figure that out."

"And winning trips is an answer?"

"Until I joined my groups and started winning contests I just went back and forth to work. I like to have a routine, but it never seemed enough. So I'd change my routine at home. I'd eat dinner on a table in front of the TV instead of at the dining room table. Things like that. Until one day I didn't want to get out of bed. And I thought of Mama killing herself. For years I never let myself think of it."

Alarmed, Rosie stared at her.

"'I'm dead,' I kept thinking. 'I'm already dead.'"

"When was this?"

"A few years ago. Before Daddy died. I thought everything was going along fine and then I knew I was dead."

Rosie wanted to take her hand but something in Deb's expression warned her not to make the gesture.

"There's no place in this world for thirty-eight-year-old virgins."

"I didn't know," Rosie said feebly.

"Why would you? We never talked about anything important. And I'm not blaming you. We were all dead."

The words sounded rehearsed to Rosie, but Deb appeared to find comfort in them. Did all of the people in her group talk this way?

"You were living with Benyoub, or Serge, or that other Arab, I don't remember his name, but somehow I knew you were dead too."

"No," Rosie said, "I wasn't dead. You're wrong."

"I know what I know."

"We shouldn't be here. Leave Mama in peace."

"We owe her more than that. We never listened. Never made her talk."

"We were children, Deb."

"We let her die, for years, because all along she was dying in front of us."

Rosie looked away.

"Listen to me. First the Hungarians rounded up the Jews in the countryside, in the small towns and villages. They were deported first. Then they began deporting the Jews from Budapest, in 1944."

Rosie shut her eyes.

"Are you listening to me?"

"Yes, Deb. I studied history too."

"Mama lived it."

Rosie sighed.

"1944 was late in the war, so most of the Hungarian Jews who survived came from Budapest. Lucky Mama. If she'd been born in a small village she'd have been gassed earlier."

"What do you want me to say?" asked Rosie.

"Whatever you feel."

"I don't like Jews. Or Christians. Or Muslims. I don't trust any of them. 'My God's better than your God' — all that superiority sickens me."

"What do you think's better?"

"People should leave each other alone. Stop judging."

"Will you come with me to see Mama's building?"

"Yes," Rosie said, exhausted. She broke the fig cookie into pieces and tossed it to a cluster of pigeons that had gathered near their bench. They pounced immediately.

The sisters made their way through the dead streets of the old ghetto, passing one run-down apartment building after another along Király utca. Few Jews lived here now, and the streets that once meant sanctuary, and were known as a center of Jewish life, had become home to gypsies and new immigrants; there wasn't a prayer shawl or earlock in sight. Yet the bleak stone buildings looked as if they still hadn't adjusted; unlike their counterparts in Paris that seemed to embrace new tenants with ease, these belonged to another time.

"That's it, over there," Deb said, pointing.

They stopped in front of number 13 and read the name *Gozsdu udvar* carved on the lintel of the building.

"It's huge," Rosie said. "I didn't expect anything like this."

The somber decaying building was actually a complex of seven parallel inner courtyards paved with yellow bricks, laid out so that it was impossible to see to the far end.

"Which courtyard was Mama's?" asked Rosie, as they entered the first one through a rusty art nouveau gate that appeared permanently open, almost welcoming demolition.

"I'm not sure," Deb said, looking at the address she'd written down. "It doesn't say."

They continued walking, and the light around them seemed to fade gradually. In the middle courtyard stood several discarded automobile tires, painted green and filled with earth, in which someone had planted bright red geraniums. From here on the courtyards began to narrow and darken.

"She probably lived in the last one," Rosie said.

"Why?" Deb folded the paper and returned it to her purse.

"They were poor people and it has the smallest courtyard."

"I don't like this place," Deb said. "It gives me the creeps."

"It's not that bad."

"You just like old buildings."

"Maybe. I like this one. It must have been something, once." Serge would have liked it as well.

"You've lived in Paris too long. There's no point in being sentimental about ratty old buildings."

Rosie peered into one of the dirty windows on the ground floor and watched as two elderly men, wearing white shirts without neckties, sat, heads bent, over ancient sewing machines. She smiled to herself. She had begun to enjoy the day after all and didn't feel a need to remind Deb that she had arranged this particular sentimental journey.

"Think of what this would have been like when it was filled with horsedrawn wagons and . . ."

Deb looked at her, surprised. "I wish we knew her courtyard."

"It's not important. Even if you knew the apartment number, and we found it, and someone let us in, you still wouldn't know what the rooms were like, or where Mama used to sleep. You'd have more questions than you came with. This is enough, Deb. It's better like this."

"There are so many things I want to know, and no one to talk to. If Uncle Aladar didn't have Alzheimer's I'd visit him, and you know I said I'd never set foot in Pittsburgh again after Daddy died."

"I know, you already said that. Just be glad we're here seeing this."

Deb frowned.

Something in the quality of the light seemed familiar to Rosie, almost comforting. She would have liked to spend the afternoon by herself in a corner of the courtyard watching people come and go. She even had a vague memory of her mother describing the courtyards to her when she was a small child, home sick from school. Elza sat by her bedside, talking in almost a whisper, while Rosie listened intently, for her mother never spoke of Europe, that place of unimaginable evils.

"It's not what I expected," Deb said.

For a moment Rosie thought of telling Deb her memory, but it wasn't clear enough. Confused, incomplete, like her cathedral dream. But Elza had certainly not told her anything like that.

"Are you going to take some pictures?" Rosie asked.

"I don't know. The light's not very good."

"Take one for me."

"Here?"

"Anywhere. This would be fine."

While Deb took out her camera, Rosie walked to the edge of the courtyard. She put her right hand on one of the crumbling stucco walls. She felt that she was being observed but didn't mind. Looking up into the filthy windows, she knew they opened from coffin-sized rooms. Elza had rarely spoken a word of Hungarian to her children, but with Uncle Aladar she sometimes did, and Rosie had been fascinated. The sickbed memory seemed to want to return: Hadn't Elza called her *drágam,* which meant my dear one, my darling?

"Smile!" Deb called out, waving, as she held the camera up to her eye.

Dear darling dead Mother, come for me.

16

$\mathcal{A}$s Rosie unlocked the apartment door a sense of dread overcame her. She wanted to tell Serge about Budapest, and the way Deb had dragged her from one Jewish site to another — whatever the guidebooks selected as worthy — but she would never see him again. The fact of it left her staggering: rootless, homeless. Why should she call this old building her home? No one makes a home alone, and claims to the contrary ought to be distrusted. The years before Serge had taught her that much. Blundering along, she had tired of her own company.

Stepping into the dark living room, Rosie fumbled for a lamp. Serge, of course, would have taken her suitcase at once, greeting her with kisses and wine.

Light filled the room and it took a moment for Rosie to believe what she saw. Books had been turned out of their shelves into heaps on the floor, the sofa cushions beside them; the television and Serge's stereo were gone.

She stood unable to move. Silence enveloped the apartment like an army of occupation, and her mouth went dry. She knew the intruder had left days ago.

The heavy pewter candlesticks, bought in a Marseilles

fleamarket, were missing, and her favorite Algerian pottery lay smashed to pieces, as if an impatient hand had swept them aside in its search.

Trembling, Rosie walked toward the bedroom, stopping at the door. The bureau drawers hung open, as did the closet door, and clothes were dumped in the middle of the bed. Yet several museum reproductions of pre-Columbian artifacts remained on the oak sideboard — the intruder had an eye for objects of little value.

Rosie crossed the room gingerly. Her jewelry box stood open, the few good pieces taken. She closed her eyes and sighed. No one had touched the antique mirror above the bureau.

Back in the living room she noticed that a handful of newspaper clippings had fallen on the floor, articles that Serge had stuffed inside books or record sleeves. By now she had seen the worst, and she told herself to stay calm. It was too late for anything else.

She telephoned the police, certain they would be useless, and then called Thierry. Renée answered, saying that he'd gone to a union meeting. She promised to come over right away: "I'm already out the door."

Rosie straightened the sofa cushions and, still wearing her raincoat, sat down in the mess. She wished that she hadn't telephoned anyone. My new life, she thought.

The room belonged to her, yet it seemed to have nothing to do with her either. Disloyal, almost, after Serge's death, their apartment hadn't registered the slightest change; it took an intruder for that.

Why, she wondered, had Serge saved all those clippings?

Half an hour later Renée arrived. It amused Rosie to see that she'd dressed as if they were off to a party, her scarfs and jewelry and makeup a kind of protection. But she knew what she looked good in.

Renée surveyed the apartment before hugging Rosie. "We both need a drink," she said.

"I don't know what there is," Rosie answered, going into the kitchen. Phoning the Roussels had been a mistake. She wanted to be by herself.

"There's some brandy," she said. "And calvados."

"Calvados," Renée called, folding her coat over the back of Serge's chair.

Rosie brought the bottle and two glasses into the living room. At fifteen her favorite book had been Erich Maria Remarque's *Arch of Triumph,* in which the doomed lovers always drank calvados. She had never shaken the association: the name still evoked a world of people tossing back their liquor over zinc bars or small marble café tables. "If Serge was an alcoholic," Rosie said, putting down the glasses, "why didn't I know it?"

"Maybe you didn't want to see. And it became part of your relationship."

Rosie poured a larger drink for Renée than for herself. "What do you mean? That he had to drink in order to live with me?"

"No. But sometimes people see what they want. You know that."

"Did you know he was an alcoholic?"

Sipping, Renée nodded. "I'll help you clean up," she offered.

"The police should see it first," Rosie said, sighing at the mess that surrounded them. "I don't know when they'll get here."

"The police!" exclaimed Renée. "They won't do anything."

"I know. But it's an automatic reaction — someone breaks into your house and you call the police."

"That's because you're an American," Renée said.

Rosie sighed. Renée had never spoken to her like that when Serge was alive. "Why do you say that?"

"Americans have more faith in bureaucracy."

The last thing Rosie wanted was to sit around discussing the American character. "I don't know," she said, rubbing her thumb against her glass. "I haven't lived there in years. But I brought you and Thierry something from Budapest. A bottle of Tokay."

"Thank you," Renée nodded. "I remember Budapest as a beautiful city."

"Yes," Rosie said, deciding to leave it at that. Serge would have wanted to hear all about Deb, and how it felt to visit the place where her mother once lived, but Renée would only tolerate her stories. "I wish Serge was here."

Renée emptied her glass.

"The days are all the same now," Rosie said. "But Sundays are really bad."

"I have bad days too. Painful days."

Rosie took the bottle and poured more calvados into Renée's glass. "You don't have to stay until the police come. I'll be fine."

"Thierry said he told you about us."

Rosie stared into her glass. Renée's hooded eyes always seemed scornful to her.

"That we haven't slept together in years."

"He told me. Do you mind?"

"That he told you? No. It's a fact. You may as well know."

"Serge never mentioned it."

"We miss him a lot."

"Why did Thierry tell me? It's not important, but I couldn't help wondering."

"Perhaps he thought it would bring us closer."

"But you don't think it will," Rosie said, measuring the effect of her words.

"No," Renée said pensively. "I don't see why it should. You look offended."

"I'm not certain what I feel. It's strange, that's all. Here I thought the two of you were happy and . . ."

"But we are happy," Renée interrupted.

"Then I don't understand."

Renée looked as if she were about to say something but Rosie quickly added, "I know, it's because I'm an American."

"Well," Renée said, laughing, "I was about to say that."

Rosie looked at her intently. Thierry, she felt, was unhappy; perhaps she'd always sensed it. "With Serge dead, it's like stepping out of one life into another."

Renée continued nursing her drink. Finally she said, " I can't imagine it."

The two women waited for the police, who arrived in less than an hour. After filling out a report, they cautioned Rosie to keep a list of all serial numbers on electronics. Renée offered to return the next evening and help with the apartment, but Rosie declined. Renée's sympathy made her feel apprehensive. As soon as she left, Rosie thought of all the things she couldn't tell Renée. Elza, she now saw, had had a life before coming to Pittsburgh, and a new country, a husband, a family, couldn't stop the pain of it. Nothing could: Rosie and Deb were only part of a life they didn't understand.

That night Rosie slept fitfully, setting a pattern for the coming weeks. She tossed, watched the clock, stared at the ceiling. It had been years since she'd slept like this, on her right side, with one hand pressed between her legs. Shadows played around her bed, Serge's bed. Their bed. Her life had absolutely no point. She might get up and brew some chamomile tea, then realize that she had never really liked it, that it was Serge who said it helped him to sleep.

Days passed without anyone speaking to her about trade unions or the party. She bought newspapers but never read them. And, after noticing that she'd lost another small clump of hair behind her left ear, she threw out the medicated shampoo. She was, she knew, afraid of many things. But the mechanics of living kept pulling her forward. She approached each day as if it were one of her classes, repeating the exercises by rote, without going below the surface. A monkey could do my job, she thought. Any reasonably trained monkey. Her students were monkeys too, repeating after her mindless requests for directions, the time of day, the cost of an item they might want to purchase, while she waited to correct their accents. "Not a French *t*," she might say, "but an English one. Softer. Like this." And she repeated the sound in question as if her life depended on it, all the while remembering Serge.

Serge, who liked to say that he no longer read books with more than two hundred pages, although she didn't believe it.

Serge, who liked to bring her small surprises from his daily wanderings: an antique tortoise-shell comb, a pot of rosemary, two trays for making madeleines (still unused), a small figurine of a Chinese pug.

Whom she had let die.

At night, after she returned home from school, Rosie would sit in the dark living room, ignoring the telephone, which rang less frequently now. She would take food from the freezer, hold the icy package to her face, leave it to defrost in the sink. She often made pasta with garlic and olive oil and would take a bowl of it to the sofa. She would stuff herself with the warm greasy noodles until she became all mouth: a hole against the world. Stuff it down.

A letter arrived from Mme Deneau, which she left unopened for days. "Naturally," Madame wrote, there were inquiries about Serge's estate. Estate — Rosie had to laugh. Would they want his old clothes? Another letter arrived, this time from Odile. She threw it unopened into the garbage. She hadn't yet cleaned up the apartment after the robbery.

One morning, while heading to her first student, Rosie passed a busy corner where people stood outside a fruit market, choosing from large baskets of apples and potatoes. It was a pleasant, bright November day, with a hint of the coming winter in the air. People buzzed to each other with sounds of excitement, happiness. Waiting for the streetlight to change, Rosie watched as an elderly woman — Chinese? Vietnamese? — took an orange from a basket, examined it intently, set it back and picked another, scrutinized this one, looked back at the pile of glistening fruit. We don't matter, Rosie thought. Whatever we tell ourselves. People are inconsequential — whether they live or die makes no difference. Of what value were the lives in her building, or the lives anywhere in Paris, in all of France? Across the entire world? Maybe you feel connected to five, six people at any time. Out of the whole world. How many over a lifetime? The sheer pointlessness of human effort numbed her. All that longing, those dreams, plans, aspirations. Hopes. What did they matter? Beside the old woman, that almost-corpse, that skeleton still wearing its bag of skin, two middle-aged men smiled at each other. Smiling at what? Foolish, indecent. One man touched the shoulder of the second, and then Rosie saw them smile at a woman who moved between them. She wore a fur coat, even though the weather made it unnecessary. She smiled back, opening her red mouth wide enough so that Rosie could see two rows of sharp teeth. She wore a thick brown pelt over her skin. The Asian woman was still studying oranges, now holding several in the crook of her elbow. The pelted woman —

years younger, probably French, with too much paint on her face — casually reached into the same basket of oranges. The grandma, the crone, jumped back, dropping an orange from her elbow. No one bent to claim it.

Rosie stepped into the street, traffic moving past her, desperate to flee them.

On every side walking corpses surrounded her. They moved, made sounds, pushed ahead, as if they had no idea that they lacked any meaning or permanence.

"Madame?" a voice asked.

Rosie moved with the herd across the boulevard.

"Madame?" it repeated.

Rosie turned to see a small, elderly man tap her arm. She wiped her face, which was wet with tears.

"Are you all right?" he asked.

She thought she recognized him: one of Serge's friend's from the newspaper office.

"Yes, I'm fine."

"I've seen you before," he said, as they stood by the curb.

He barely came to Rosie's shoulder, and she guessed that he was closing on ninety. He seemed to be made of tissue paper, and held a cane in his right hand.

"With Serge Deneau," he said. "I used to help him sell newspapers. At the Stalingrad rotunda."

"Yes." Rosie nodded, drawing away.

"Please remember me to him," he said, smiling gallantly. She nodded.

In the subway Rosie found a telephone and called the switchboard at school, canceling her students for the day. The flu, she explained. Some kind of flu. Then she hurried back to her apartment. The postman had already been, leaving several bills, a letter from Deb, another from her cousin Joel.

Back in her bed, Rosie tried to distract herself by remembering Budapest. Soiled velvet chairs in the hotel.

Casinos on Buda Hill that took only Deutschmarks, and drunken Germans gambling as fast as possible while her sister lost fifty dollars. Endless glass pastry cases. The thick, soupy, polluted air, stinking of gasoline. And Deb's disappointment: had she expected their mother's apartment to be some grand residence on the banks of the Danube? Rosie counted off details, aware that important ones eluded her. She could not recall the series of courtyards at Gozsdu udvar with any exactness, and tried to walk through the city in her mind, from the hotel to the Liberty Bridge, across to . . . where? . . . she remembered none of the street names.

I'm crazy, she told herself. An idiot. A fool. A bag of blood and bones.

She reached for Deb's letter, opening it slowly, preparing for a blast. On the last night in Budapest they had argued bitterly, Deb insisting that Rosie's lack of interest in the Holocaust proved her to be the worst of all Jews, an anti-Semite. Rosie had shouted back that their mother wanted to put the camps behind her, and reading about Auschwitz wouldn't bring them closer to Elza. Exasperated, Deb had stomped out of their room. An hour later Rosie found her in a bar off the lobby, where they sat in muddled silence drinking a sweet apricot brandy that made Rosie sick to her stomach.

Deb's kind of evening, Rosie now thought. Full of guilt and recriminations. Their father would have loved it.

She opened the letter and read it with relief. Deb never mentioned their argument, or the tension between them during the week. Instead, she regretted that she hadn't yet mastered her new camera, for all the film she'd used had turned out to be blank, and then urged Rosie to move to New York.

Rosie could see it all clearly: they would enter contests together, and haunt restaurants where old Yiddish writers took their meals. She shuddered. As a postscript Deb had written, "Think about what it means to be a Jew," echoing their father.

Joel's letter puzzled her more, for she hadn't heard from him since Morris's funeral, and she scanned it quickly. Deb had told him about Serge's death — Rosie felt certain she'd never mentioned Serge to him — and he wanted to suggest that she consider returning to Pittsburgh, her home. He was well connected, he had a good network, he knew he could help find her a decent job. Americans belonged in America. As head of the family he had to tell her this.

Torn between annoyance and pity, Rosie crumpled the page into a ball. Joel must torture his children nightly, doting on them. *"I know what's best for you,"* she could hear him say, *"as head of the family."* Patriarch, fixer, sainted father. Clean-shaven, self-assured bag of shit and piss. He must be Serge's age now. Why hadn't he died instead?

One day she would write to Joel; he deserved a reply. A patriarch needs someone to lord over. Pittsburgh! she'd say. No one chooses to live in Pittsburgh, unless you're born there, planted to die there — if you don't escape first. But when he convinced Deb to come back, she'd consider his offer. A safe bet, that. Fat chance. Maybe they could buy back their childhood house, although she suspected Joel would say the old neighborhood had "gone Black." Nonetheless, she and Deb would insist on that house alone, keep a kosher kitchen, and age together like two amiable spinsters. "The Kamin girls," that's how we'd be known. Me, the older one, the one with the walker. The one who had lived in France for a time.

She pulled the blanket around her chin, rolled over onto her stomach, buried her face in the pillow. The sheets no longer held Serge's scent: unfamiliar, disloyal things. She would never hear his footstep in another room of the apartment, never wake to find his arm cradling her.

He had lied about his health.

Let himself die.

Refused her help.

Left her alone.

They had both been fools.

Rosie pushed her face deeper into the pillow. Serge had abandoned her. He'd been careless, gone away. Just like her mother.

On the weekend Elza had killed herself, Deb was away at college, where she lived, while Rosie had gone on a peace march in Washington. Uncle Aladar had asked Morris to accompany him on a short business trip to Buffalo, where they had to stay overnight. For the first time in twenty-five years Elza was left alone. Instead of watching television, enjoying a quiet bath, or the brief freedom from her family, instead of having a sandwich for dinner rather than cooking a hot meal, and sleeping late the next morning, Elza had taken an overdose of Seconal, as if she'd been waiting for the opportunity for years.

When Morris returned late Sunday afternoon he found her body on the floor beside their double bed. He telephoned Deb at once, but couldn't locate Rosie, who was still marching in Washington. She returned home on Monday to a house in the midst of funeral plans. Elza had left a note saying "I'm sorry," nothing more.

Rosie pulled away from the pillow, gasping for air. She breathed a scent of death and betrayal.

Serge belonged at her side; Elza should be alive somewhere in Pittsburgh, cleaning up after lunch, planning the rest of her day.

I won't forgive you. I won't forgive you. I won't.

17

*H*ALF A DOZEN LARGE cardboard boxes lined the wall in Rosie's bedroom as if she were packing to move. On one of them she had left an untouched bowl of muesli, which looked to her like poisoned rat food.

"If you had to come back, which would you rather be, a man or a woman?" Thierry asked.

Rosie handed him a pair of Serge's trousers to put in the last box. "I wouldn't want to come back," she said. "The idea of reincarnation gives me the creeps."

"That's not fair." Thierry looked at her as if she'd cheated.

"Why? Because you have to re-think your choice? The trouble with reincarnation is all that ego. In a past life you're always a Christian martyr or Spanish dancer or famous yogi. No one ever says 'In a previous life I made gloves, and they weren't very good ones.'"

"Still, reincarnation's better than the afterlife."

"You can have them both." She took a heavy black sweater from the closet and held it up. "This might fit you, and it's practically new."

Thierry closed the box and smiled awkwardly. "It might."

Rosie hadn't answered her telephone for almost a month, since returning from Budapest, and Thierry finally dropped by the apartment to see what was wrong. To avoid talking, she asked him to help her pack Serge's belongings. He had been dead for three months now.

"I had a visit from Jean Berthelot," she said. "The other day. You remember, Serge's old friend. The man who came here with Odile."

Thierry reached for the black sweater and pulled it on over his head. "It is my size, isn't it?"

"Looks fine," Rosie answered. "Really."

"What did he want?"

"Apparently Odile's on the warpath. I get a headache just thinking of her. She has some notion that Serge left a huge estate. She's seen a lawyer, and Jean wanted to warn me. He thinks she can be dangerous."

Removing the sweater, Thierry set it on a pile of clothes on the foot of the bed. "There couldn't have been much," he reflected.

"Forty thousand francs," she said. Eight thousand dollars. "But you know Odile. The amazing thing is she thinks I'm a crook."

"Did Berthelot say that?"

"Not in those words. He's really very sweet, but I must have embarrassed him. I insisted on knowing what Odile had said though I could tell he didn't want to repeat things, but I wouldn't let him alone."

Thierry listened intently.

"She said I have to be watched because I'm a Jew."

"I don't believe it."

"You know Jews," Rosie said derisively. "Greedy. High-strung. That's what she thinks of me."

"Odile said that?"

"I used to tell Serge she was a monster."

"This is all so hard on you," Thierry said.

Rosie shrugged. If she concealed her feelings Thierry might stop worrying about her, and telephoning with advice. Whenever he called she expected him to ask for Serge.

Thierry crossed the room and put a hand on her shoulder. "You can count on me . . ." he said.

"I'm all right. It's probably a good thing to pack up Serge's clothes. Though it's not like I need any reminders."

". . . if there's anything else I can do." He stood closer.

She looked at him uncomfortably, surprised by the intimate tone of his voice.

"I'll be fine."

"But you have needs," he said.

She drew back.

"Renée and I talked about it. And she thinks it would be a good thing."

"What?"

"Renée thinks it would be best for you. Eventually you're going to feel sexual again. Maybe not now, but you will. And it would be better with a friend than a stranger."

"I'm not hearing this," she said.

"Don't be upset, Rosie." His face held only friendly solicitousness.

"Have I gone crazy or something? Just because you and Renée don't sleep together doesn't mean I should take her place."

"It's got nothing to do with me and Renée."

"Oh, come on. You're making me angry. I think you'd better go."

"I'm sorry, Rosie, I didn't mean to upset you."

"Well you have."

"I . . ."

"Serge's best friend," she cut him off contemptuously.

"I really care for you. Or I wouldn't have brought it up."

She looked into his eyes and guessed that he meant what he said. "If you care for me you'll go now."

"I don't want you to be angry."

"I want one thing. Just one thing. Serge. That's all."

"You have to keep on living."

"Don't tell me that. Please."

"Maybe we should talk about this."

"Thierry, please, just go." She sat down on the bed and looked away from him. Rosie knew she had never flirted with him, never encouraged such attention, even in jest. Thierry should have seen that she needed a friend who'd cared for Serge, and not a lover — no, she thought, lover isn't the right word — sex partner.

"I hate to leave you upset. I'll phone you later."

She didn't reply.

"Tomorrow," he said.

She picked up the alarm clock from the bedside table and thought about throwing it.

"Rosie?"

"Leave me alone. Okay? I don't feel gracious or thankful or understanding." She spoke without facing him.

"I'm sorry," he called.

As soon as he left Rosie began to shake. What timing, she thought bitterly. Earlier that week Deb had written again, asking, "Are you saving yourself for another Frenchman?"

Deb should have liked Renée, the only person Rosie knew who would greet dinner guests at the front door while holding a butcher's knife in her hand. She tried to imagine Renée and Thierry sitting in their white apartment discussing her needs. Which one of them had come up with the idea? Renée, because she'd slept with Serge a few times years ago? It made no sense. The four of them had spent countless evenings together, and now the Roussels wanted to offer up Thierry as some kind of sex therapist. They'd gone fucking crazy.

We're all fools. Vermin.

Rosie saw that she had no reason to live; not another day. She closed her eyes and tried to imagine life flowing out of her body. At first light-headed, then free, she would simply drift away from the world. Her body would seem to be floating until she realized that she'd left it behind. She would be lighter than air. The world would vanish, disintegrate. No color or sound or light. Names or histories. Better than sleep, for she would never have to return.

Serge's razor blades were still in the bathroom cabinet, but the thought of them frightened Rosie, who dreaded the sight of blood. And she could never throw herself from the roof, or in front of a car or a moving train. Pills were the answer. Surely one of Serge's doctors would write out a prescription. That bastard Chollet would probably refuse, but Dr. Bertin, a woman, might be sympathetic. She was old enough to know that the tradition of tossing wives onto the funeral pyre had a clean logic to it. But pills would be easier.

Serge, Mama, are you waiting for me?

Rocking back and forth, she remembered nearly telling Thierry about the cathedral dream, which she'd had again. Maybe he could help her get some pills. No — he wants to fuck. What good's a corpse for that? Don't answer, Rosie. Watch it. She wanted to crush her head between her hands, stopping her thoughts.

Come with me. C'mon. Come along. Can you still be surprised? I know, life is hard.

Let me die too.

People said you were greeted on the bridge into death — untrue, impossible! Serge knew only stillness, a sweet oblivion. She had nothing to ask him, or Elza either.

Swaying, Rosie closed her eyes and heard a distant rumble of thunder. Wind blew at her, through her skin, her flesh, leaving her almost transparent, uncovering her bones. She was nothing but bones; they hummed, crooned, her bone fingers moving with the wind.

"Rosie?" a voice called out softly.

She didn't answer at first.

"Rosie?"

"I'm over here."

Serge pushed through the bushes that fringed the edge of a pond. She sat near its bank, her feet curled under her.

"Why did you leave?" he asked.

"I don't know." She tossed a pebble in the water and it splashed. Night had fallen and they were surrounded by darkness. "It's nothing, Serge, forget it, okay?"

"All right."

They sat together quietly, feeling awkward.

"I love you, Rosie, you know that, don't you?"

She didn't answer but reached for another pebble. He took her hand.

"I hated it back there, with all of them," she said.

"No one will guess we've talked if . . ."

She looked away. "Weren't you expecting me?"

"No, why should I? I didn't even think of it." He took a sprig of goldenrod and tucked it into her hair, crouching closer beside her.

"It seems odd, that's all, it bothers me."

He slipped his arm over her shoulder, and her skin was cold.

"Serge?"

He leaned forward to kiss her.

"This awful place!" she cried.

Serge looked up sadly. "What did you expect?"

Her legs were white in the moonlight.

"Do you have a new lover?" he asked.

Surprised at the question, she hid her face.

"Do you?" he repeated.

When she shook her head, he reached for her chin with his hand. Their skin was sticking and she imagined herself somewhere else, distantly watching the scene.

"Love you, Rosie." She held onto his head. "Love you," he whispered while she watched for an intruder over his shoulder. "Love you."

Rosie fell on her side, on the bed, her eyes streaming.

Let me die, let me die.

There was a loud knock on the apartment door. Rosie ignored it, at first; she didn't want to see Thierry again, or anyone else. But the knocking persisted.

She navigated her way through the boxes that lined the living room, one filled with broken pieces of pottery left from the robbery, another with Serge's books, a third with old magazines and newspaper clippings. Unsorted letters and bills were spread over the coffee table, along with Serge's notebooks.

"Who is it?" Rosie called.

"Hamed Benali."

"Yes?" she called through the closed door.

"May I see you?"

Rosie opened the door slowly. Hamed looked bigger, taller, in his dark overcoat. "Yes?" she said.

Hamed surveyed the apartment. "Are you moving?"

"No," Rosie answered, without explanation.

"Aren't you going to invite me in?"

He seemed to be eyeing the sofa, and Rosie could see him sitting there, stretched out like a plump black cat, his hands clasped behind his head, his legs casually crossed, one foot moving about in the air as if pleased with itself. Poor Thierry, she thought, he didn't like being a seducer.

Unlike Hamed, or Ben. They enjoyed their bodies and needed women to make them come alive. Thierry had never grown up, that was the only thing wrong with him. And now he would disappoint Renée again. She wondered if she should call him to apologize. The bastard.

"No," she said, watching Hamed flinch. "I'm just going out. I want some fresh air. But you can walk with me if you like."

"It's about to rain," he said.

"I'll take an umbrella."

"Are you afraid to be alone with me?"

If men weren't so crude, she would almost think all widows gave off an inviting scent. Yet men and women deserved each other. Recently in the lunch room at school one of the teachers had recommended seeing old lovers "once, for old time's sake, if you're crawling the walls."

"My coat's in the other room," Rosie said.

Hamed remained in the doorway while Rosie pulled on her raincoat and found her umbrella and purse. He had obviously been taking her measure while they talked, and Rosie resented his presumption. Serge's death seemed to have unleashed all the horrors of her past.

"I thought I'd walk along the canal," she said, returning to the living room.

Hamed nodded patiently as she tied a scarf around her head, babushka-style.

Outside of her building, they walked unhurriedly under a khaki-colored sky. The wind blew in gusts, and light drops of rain hit Rosie's face, but she didn't seem to notice. "We can take a shortcut," Rosie suggested.

Hamed stuffed his large gloveless hands into his coat pockets. In a few weeks it would be Christmas.

It took them a quarter of an hour to reach the canal. On summer evenings Rosie and Serge had often strolled there to watch the barges slip through the locks. Children usually crowded the embankment while men played *boules* or *pétanque* as daylight faded. This afternoon only a lone jogger ran past them. In the distance, the canal became a gray ribbon.

They passed a low wooden bench but Rosie continued to walk. The wind had died down. "Why did you want to see me?" she asked. "Is it about Ben?"

"Yes," Hamed replied.

Rosie didn't look up. She had no reason to believe him.

"I telephoned several times but you never answered," he added.

She supposed that Hamed could have gotten her number from Ben, or even from the telephone directory. Perhaps he meant to apologize for his last outburst. Yet Rosie couldn't recall him ever apologizing before.

"Has Ben phoned you?"

"No," she said. "You gave him my message?"

"Of course I did. What do you take me for?"

"I'm sorry, Hamed."

"How much did you loan him?"

"That's not the point."

"Then why did you come looking for Ben?"

"He was there when Serge went into the hospital. I guess I wanted to talk about Serge . . ."

"Has he paid you back yet?"

"I'm sure he will."

"It's a matter of pride," Hamed said. "Pride in his word."

"I don't think he sees it that way. And it wasn't that much."

"He makes me ashamed."

Rosie hated the fact that she'd lied about the amount to protect Benyoub. "Do you know where he is?" she asked. "I haven't thought of him recently."

"He moves around a lot."

"It's all so mysterious. Like he's a criminal. That's not the Ben I knew."

Hamed didn't reply.

"Difficult, yes," she continued.

"Benyoub has to live his life," Hamed replied.

"Is that supposed to sound mystical?" Rosie continued to avoid his face, not knowing what else to do. Hamed, the bully with feelings, troubled her. Perhaps his motives were honest.

"Why did you stay in Paris?" he asked. "I thought you'd have gone back to America long ago."

"I'm the original Wandering Jew."

"America's better than France," he said with conviction.

"How do you know? You've never been there."

She looked at him now, and he frowned, saying, "The French hate everyone who isn't."

She shook her head.

"You think I'm wrong?"

"Nobody wants to be where they are. When Serge was alive I thought if only he had a job that he liked, and we could get a bigger apartment . . ." She stopped at the picture of unclouded happiness.

Hamed turned up the collar of his coat and took the umbrella from her, tilting it against the rain.

"This afternoon, just before you came, a good friend, a married man, someone I trust, offered to sleep with me. As if he'd be doing me a favor."

"He's a bad man," Hamed said.

From the look on his face Rosie guessed that he was clenching his teeth. The thought amused her. "No, he isn't. That's the problem. I'm very angry at him, but he's not a bad man. That's too simple."

"Such sophistications always get you in trouble. Some things are simple."

She tried not to smile.

"Then you admit I'm right," he added.

"No. I don't." She felt weary, drained. At birth people's tongues should be cut out. Let them torment each other with letters — you can choose to ignore a letter. She would get the pills somehow.

"I think you don't like to admit defeat," Hamed observed.

"I have to go now," Rosie said abruptly.

Hamed moved to follow her.

"No, I need to do some errands alone. When you see Ben . . . oh . . . never mind . . ."

Hamed gave her the umbrella and watched as she ran across the street.

Back in her apartment Rosie kicked off her shoes and tossed her coat on the bed. Some of her blouses were mixed up with a pile of Serge's shirts, and she pulled out a yellow one that she rarely wore, its color intense, even harsh. She reached for a pair of scissors on the bedside table and slowly cut out a six-pointed star, about five inches in diameter, from the back of the blouse. Then she found a needle and thread in the tin cookie box she jokingly called a sewing kit. After several tries she threaded the needle, reached for the star, and sewed it onto the breast of her coat.

18

ROSIE SET ABOUT GATHERING pills. Her mother had used them, and she found the thought comforting. An afternoon in the library taught her that antidepressants and a bottle of red wine would do the job, since doctors no longer prescribed barbiturates with abandon. Yet Rosie never seemed surprised at how easy it was to convince several doctors that she needed an antidepressant; it was as easy as ordering pâté at her favorite charcuterie: "I want" suddenly became magic words. She decided to take the pills on the Sunday before Christmas, after visiting Serge's grave the previous afternoon. The plan had an elegance that pleased her.

During her free evenings after work, Rosie began straightening bureau drawers, discarding old papers. In the bottom of one drawer she found a brown envelope with a photograph from a French magazine that she'd taped to her mirror during her first months in Paris, in case she became homesick. Censored by American newspapers, it showed a Vietnamese woman, naked to the waist, with sores covering her shoulders and breasts. In her arms lay a dead baby. Rosie took the clipping and taped it onto her bureau mirror. She hadn't thought of the Paris peace talks in years. Deb would have to come over and take charge of the mess, but there would be a small inheritance to compensate for her troubles. Rosie felt calm, distant, like an afterthought, or ice cubes melting in the bottom of a glass. Serge had committed the unpardonable sin of dying, yet here she sat, with one of his favorite books, Flaubert's Egyptian journal, about to thumb through the pages.

When Rosie began wearing her raincoat with the badly stitched yellow star, she noticed that people seemed not to sit beside her on the subway. She didn't mind, she actually preferred the extra space. An occasional angry reaction on someone's face might have been directed at another person; after all, most people walking along in the streets looked angry, troubled, or preoccupied.

At the end of the second week Rosie found a message in her mailbox at school, asking her to stop at her supervisor's office. She wondered if a student had complained about her, some nasty middle-aged businessman who wanted to lay blame because his thick mind repelled the English language. Possibly M. Odoul, yes. Rosie looked at her watch. Twenty minutes before her first student, time enough for complaints.

Mme Léonie Serreau, a cat-faced widow with dyed orange hair, had been guarding the corridors of Continental since it opened in the late 1950s. Her expression suggested that she embodied the school's history, although no one else shared her belief. She had a cramped, dark, windowless office in the back of the building, across from the men's room.

Rosie found the door ajar and knocked softly.

It opened slowly, dramatically. "Ah! Mme Kamin, you've come to see me."

Rosie waited to be invited in.

"You're early this morning."

"I have an early student, at eight o'clock. Before he goes to his office."

"Yes," she paused. "Of course. But please come in, sit down."

Rosie entered the office and took a seat at the small table that served as a desk.

Mme Serreau closed the door at once. Wearing an old, loose, gray wool sweater and skirt, and a single strand of coral beads, she moved as if her ill-fitting clothes belonged to someone else. Cigarette ashes had left small marks on the front of the sweater. "We must talk seriously," she began, still standing. "We are, of course, aware of your recent loss."

Surprised, Rosie leaned forward. She'd never had a personal conversation with Mme Serreau in twenty years of teaching at Continental.

"And, of course, we understand that these last months have been difficult for you."

"Is something wrong, Madame?" asked Rosie.

Not to be hurried, Léonie Serreau lowered her head for a moment, as if to pay her respects. Serge had, after all, been a Frenchman. "And we've made allowances," she continued.

"Allowances?" repeated Rosie. She thought she could see her supervisor's lips quiver slightly.

"But it is time to stop."

Rosie considered this as Mme Serreau settled at her desk, in front of a framed reproduction of one of Gauguin's Brittany peasant women in an elaborate white headdress.

"You mustn't be a pessimist," Mme Serreau offered.

"Pessimist, optimist — they're just words . . ."

"You're still a young woman." She pushed a student's paper to one side of her desk.

"Nothing divides up like that," Rosie continued.

"You have to trust in God."

Rosie looked at her blankly. "I don't understand what you mean."

"Don't you believe in God?"

"God!" She made a fist with one hand. "Don't tell me about any loving, personal God. Not after the way Serge suffered."

"There have been several complaints," Mme Serreau said, quickly changing the subject.

Rosie nodded.

"About your yellow star."

"That!" Rosie cried plaintively.

"May I ask why you're wearing it?"

Rosie kept her eyes fixed on the woman's face.

"My question isn't a personal one," Mme Serreau added.

"There's no simple answer," Rosie said.

"Well, you must understand that some of our teachers and students have found it anti-Semitic."

"But I'm a Jew!" exclaimed Rosie. "For God's sake . . ."

"Yes, of course. I'm only telling you what people are saying. And we can't have controversy, we can't have unhappy students." She paused, as if she were accustomed to a life among savages.

"Yes?" Rosie asked.

"So I must ask you — we must ask you — to remove the star."

"I'll have to think about that," Rosie said. She would not apologize.

"Madame?"

Rosie looked down at the star protectively. She guessed that it resembled the first, home-made ones, and not the perfect, even shapes that manufacturers later produced in bulk.

"Have you seen a doctor?" asked Mme Serreau. Her black eyebrows moved expressively.

Rosie shook her head.

"Perhaps you need someone to talk to."

"I don't like doctors," Rosie said.

For the first time Mme Serreau smiled. "You must remove the star," she cautioned. "By the end of the day."

Any minute Rosie expected her to say that time heals all wounds, maybe even dredge up the story of a lost love as proof.

"We are not unfair," Mme Serreau said.

Rosie glanced at the door. "My student is waiting."

Nodding, Mme Serreau excused her with a firm stare.

Windbag, Rosie thought as she left the office. In twenty-four hours she would be on her way to Serge's grave; in forty-eight, she would take the pills. Next Monday morning someone else could help M. Odoul practice the future tense.

On Saturday Rosie took an early train from the Gare Montparnasse to La Ferté-Bernard, where she planned to hire a taxi to drive her to Serge's village. She had no thought of telephoning Mme Deneau or Odile, and hoped that there would be no accidental meeting at the graveside. Jean Berthelot had called again, saying that he would be pleased to accompany her if she wanted to visit Serge, but Rosie thanked him and declined, saying that she wasn't ready to see his grave again. Apparently Odile only wanted any old family photographs that Serge might have kept in the apartment. Well, she'd have them soon enough.

Settling in her train seat, Rosie fumbled through her string bag for the volume of Flaubert she'd brought to read, like anyone with a few quiet hours to kill. In the bottom of her purse were two bottles of antidepressants, a secret hoard. I'm getting out of here soon, she thought. Nearly all the early-morning passengers looked like well-bred Parisians overdressed for *le weekend*. With Christmas looming, several of them carried bags filled with gaily wrapped presents. They seemed absorbed in themselves, like swans or peacocks. Rosie crossed her legs, opened her purse to check on the pills — yes, two bottles, still there, waiting — and picked up her book again. The couple in front of her were whispering now, then kissing. Brazenly, she thought. On display, for an audience. She looked out the window as the train slowly began to pull away from the station. At Christmas she and Serge had stayed in Paris, usually spending the day with the Roussels. A dozen people might drop by during the afternoon, Serge's friends from the party, teachers from school — especially the new ones, the strays, who hadn't yet made lives for themselves in Paris. Rosie counted backward: 1990, the young Polish woman who quit Continental after six months; 1989, Nadja and her Romanian lover, who left her for a rich Vietnamese woman; 1988, the Italian student who later killed himself . . . no . . . she didn't need memories any more. I'm getting out of here, she reminded herself. She could feel the weight of the pills on the seat beside her, a rebuke to death, a glowing invitation.

"You have no right," a male voice exclaimed, and Rosie looked up to see a bearded man in his sixties standing by her seat. An elderly woman in a black fur coat and old-fashioned black felt hat stood, weeping, several feet behind him.

"These seats aren't reserved," Rosie said.

"That!" the man said, looking at the star on her coat.

Rosie sighed.

He continued to glare at her, the rat in the garden, and she almost felt sorry for him. He wore a burgundy colored necktie embossed with small white circles, identical to one of Serge's ties still hanging in the back of the bedroom closet.

"I'm sorry," she said, exasperated by his attention. "But please mind your own business."

"This is my business." His accent was faint, probably from Central Europe.

"I'll call the porter," she said.

"They should throw you off the train."

Rosie drew back as the woman reached for her companion's arm. The young couple in the seat ahead had turned to watch the commotion, which appeared to amuse them.

"You don't belong near decent people," the man said.

Rosie wished that she were naked under her coat so that she might open it to enrage him further. She looked away, out the window again, refusing to acknowledge the star on her coat. Paris was vanishing behind them.

The man remained by her seat but Rosie ignored him, opening the Flaubert. She would ignore all memories. On October 22, 1849, Flaubert had set out from Croisset, leaving his family at the Rouen station, for the ship in Marseilles that would take him to Alexandria. An hour out of Marseilles he vomited the glass of rum he'd drunk to prevent being sick.

"You should be ashamed," the voice declared before moving away.

For the next few minutes Rosie followed Flaubert. En route to Cairo, he was calling on the Minister of Foreign Affairs in white tie and tails.

Out of here, out of here, out of here, spun her mind.

At Christmas Serge always wanted roast goose, a horrible mess to clean up. She closed her book on her thumb.

"By the end of the day," Léonie Serreau had warned.

As the train sped by the bleak wintry countryside Rosie leaned her head back against the seat and closed her eyes. Everywhere she turned life was thwarting her, demanding allegiance. Elza had worn a yellow star, and survived it, for a time. And then she'd drawn apart, Seconals in hand, to lick the wounds that intimacy gave her.

Try as she might, Rosie could barely remember her mother's funeral. Instead, she saw the dark corridor of a decaying apartment building: Gozsdu udvar. Serge would have liked it, found it sympathetic. Europe was crushed by stones.

Every August, when she and Serge had ridden the train to La Ferté-Bernard, to visit the Deneaus, they had joked about his monster sister, his monster mother, yet it never occurred to Rosie that his humor was the line of least resistance. Odile would be waiting with an unopened bottle of pear *eau de vie* and their family murk. You could almost smell the mists of early autumn. Of rot, sweet decay. Sometimes it rained and they were confined to the house with Madame and Odile. Serge, who rarely smoked, would welcome his half-sister's offer of cigarettes. At night he would lie beside Rosie, wide awake; she couldn't help him. She had failed everyone she loved. "What is it?" she'd ask, her hand on his chest. "I'd like a cigarette," he might say, or, "Don't be afraid." But he wouldn't hold out his arms. She would press her body against his. "To hell with them," he'd answer, groping for his watch on the bedside table. The window shutters would rattle.

Sighing, Rosie looked back at the Flaubert. Why, she wondered, had Serge loved this book? It was too late to ask. She thought of his empty chair, his empty half of the bed. This would be her last day of remembering.

My turn, Rosie thought. I'm next.

Once the train pulled into the railway station at La Ferté-Bernard, Rosie got off and hailed a taxi near the post office. The ride to Serge's village would take another half hour. Unlike Paris, which was filled with Christmas decorations, the countryside had a somber, midwinter mien. Several cows spotted a field to her right, and she nearly asked her driver why they weren't in a barn. But one question might lead to another, and she wanted to remain invisible. She turned away from the back of his dark, balding head.

At the cemetery Rosie asked the driver to wait, and then stepped out of the taxi. A blast of cold air hit her, and she had to steady herself.

Directly ahead, the empty cemetery looked smaller than she had remembered. She crossed the road, wishing that she'd worn boots. The ground was muddy until she reached the gravel path leading through the iron gate to the first graves; then, mud again. Since the gravestones were crowded together, Rosie needed to watch her feet as she walked — one wrong step and it would be easy to trip. Many of the crumbling old gravestones hadn't been tended, or visited, in years. She found her way to the Deneau tombstone and stood before it, staring at the new metal plaque with Serge's name. She didn't recall Odile mentioning the plaque in her letters. Wind had blown dead pine needles across the tombstone.

"Serge?" she called softly.

In the summer they might have visited the graveside together. He would have carried a few small gardening tools to remove the heavy growth of weeds, she would have brought a bouquet of flowers, perhaps a packet of seeds to scatter around the tombstone. If only she could sit beside him in her best dress, clasp his hand.

"Serge?"

The tombstone, rootless, marked grave, coffin, body. Generations of Deneaus had been buried here for a century and a half. Bare trees now made sticklike shadows in the sun over their graves. Rosie wished that she'd stopped to buy flowers in La Ferté-Bernard. She looked back at the road, at her waiting taxi. The driver was reading a newspaper, absorbed in fresh scandals. An occasional pickup truck sped past, but no one seemed to notice her.

She wanted to run down the road, cross the field, find a place to hide. In the distance the cloudless sky grew dark, but she knew that she would keep on running. The world was pulling apart, stretching as tight as it could.

Only I'm not dead, she thought.

Yet the world kept pulling apart.

The night would grow cold and damp. Soon, wisps of fog would fill the hollows alongside the road. No one would notice a lone woman walking downcast, or stop for her. She would move with the wind and the shifting fog.

She wanted to tell Serge about Thierry, about the Roussels' offer, and about Odile's lawyer and Jean Berthelot's advice. "I'm sorry," she whispered. "I shouldn't bother you. It seems I can't talk anymore without apologizing." Madame and Odile were probably getting up from a late lunch at this moment.

As wind whipped the cemetery, Rosie felt it caress her: "You know the best years of your life? When you're dead."

Simone, Jules, Aubin, Coralie, she read off their names. They meant nothing to her. Had they minded death? Edouard, Théodule, Thérèse. She might rub her hands on the tombstone, but no one would again feel the touch of their skin. In Budapest Deb had traced the carved Hebrew letters on the synagogue monument with one finger.

"I've brought some pills," Rosie said aloud. She didn't open her purse.

A grave is a kind of skin.

"Good ones," she added.

The tombstone had nothing to offer. Serge, only one of many Deneaus, would have been the first to warn: "Don't look for me in the stone."

"I won't forget you," Rosie said.

The tombstone challenged: "Go on, take the pills, if you want to."

Rosie stepped back, saying, "No matter what."

19

$\mathcal{T}$HE DESSERTS ARE VERY good here."

Rosie looked up at the waiter, distracted. He was heavy-set, and in his late twenties, with a full black beard.

"I don't want anything else," she said, surveying the remains of her half-eaten dinner: chunks of lamb, spiced rice, a yogurt sauce.

"My aunt makes them herself."

"Yes," Rosie nodded, "but I don't want anything else."

This was the first time she'd tried the Turkish restaurant, not far from the Stalingrad station. Dimly lit, its cinnamon-colored walls were hung with framed travel posters of Turkey. On each table a glass bud vase held a plastic yellow rose.

"Then I'll show you a poem," he said.

Rosie frowned. A dark blue headband held long black hair away from his round face. "I don't need poetry," she answered.

"We all need poetry," he replied.

Something about his deferential eyes made her forget how sad she felt. If not Turkish, she thought, then *maghrébin*. Perhaps from Algeria.

"May I tell you about myself?" he asked, piling her dinner plate onto a tray.

"I don't want a story."

At eleven o'clock the restaurant was nearly empty and about to close for the night.

"I'll tell you the truth."

"Would you?" Rosie asked, smiling. "I'm not sure I want that either."

"Okay," he said, rebuked.

She shrugged and took a sip of wine. She'd drunk a lot of wine with dinner, which left her feeling a bit bleary, but contented.

"But I know something's bothering you."

"Don't give it another thought," Rosie said, almost in a whisper, while brushing crumbs away from her place.

He smiled again, yet warily. "You should try some dessert."

Rosie looked out the window onto a small courtyard. It was still raining. "I'll just finish this wine."

He emptied the carafe into her glass and left her, a pasha exiled to the kitchen. The restaurant was so quiet she could have put her head on the table and fallen asleep. She yawned without bothering to cover her mouth, then slumped over the last of the wine.

During the train ride back to Paris Rosie had held one of the bottles of pills in her hand. After arriving at Gare Montparnasse, she'd taken a subway to the Opéra exit and gone into the Galeries Lafayette. The department store was about to close in half an hour, which gave enough time to find the section of women's clothes, select a raincoat and take it to the clerk. Now she wouldn't have to remove the star from the coat she was wearing. Then Rosie went home and slept for fifteen hours straight. Awaking on Sunday at noon, she looked at the bottles of pills on her bedside table and knew that she was about to fail herself, just as she'd failed her mother and Serge. On Monday morning she wore her new raincoat to school, and since it had been raining steadily for the last two weeks, told friends that she'd wanted a change. People looked encouraged by her remark, but Rosie paid no attention. She continued to carry the bottles of pills in her purse, just in case. She could always use them later.

The next days had brought two more letters from family. Deb wrote about an upcoming contest to Jamaica, and Joel wanted to tell her that next summer his eldest daughter, Elaine, would be coming to Paris for her junior year abroad, and he hoped that Rosie would keep an eye on her — since she obviously wasn't returning to Pittsburgh. What is it about death, Rosie wondered, that made her family so eager to reclaim her, like a lost treasure? There was also a postcard, enclosed in an envelope, from Benyoub; the postmark was "Algeria." Hamed had written with the news of Serge's death and Ben wanted to say that he was thinking of Rosie. In the spring, once he returned to France, he would like to invite her to dinner. He didn't mention the unpaid loan. Rosie threw all the mail on the kitchen table and prepared a lesson for her next class.

Tonight, as Rosie finished her wine, she realized that the waiter was watching her from across the room. She motioned him to bring her check, and took her wallet from her purse.

"I trust everything was to your satisfaction," he said.

She put a hundred-franc note on the tray. "If only it would stop raining," she said.

"It's getting late. If you can wait five minutes, I'll walk you to the Métro."

"I've got an umbrella," she said, reaching for her new coat on the chair beside her. She decided not to mention that her apartment was within walking distance.

"Then we'll each have one. You can't be too careful after dark."

As Rosie stood up the wine hit her. She felt dizzy and weak at her ankles.

"Please sit there and wait for me," the waiter insisted.

He went off to get his coat, returning so quickly that she didn't have time to wonder why he wasn't staying to help close for the night.

The rain hadn't let up since she'd gone into the restaurant. He opened his umbrella and held it over them protectively. "Were you born in Paris?" he asked.

"No," Rosie said. He took her arm and she leaned against him.

They walked silently. A light scent hung in the air and Rosie couldn't identify it at first. It didn't smell like Paris, this combination of pollution and mist from the canal. For a moment it made her think of ether. Rosie wrinkled her nose. No. It smelled like Pittsburgh.

"This will be my first Christmas in France," he offered.

Rosie thought of the Roussels, who had left several messages on her answering machine, asking her to join them for the holiday dinner. She felt defeated by the Christmas spirit. This would be the time to visit the desert, with only palm trees in sight.

"Your French is very good," she said.

"I write poems," he said. "But not in French."

She supposed that she should show some interest. "I've never written a poem," she said. "Is it difficult?"

"We could go back to my place," he suggested. "Until the rain stops."

Rosie didn't look at him.

"It's not far. Just another block."

Rosie veered off with him, passing the stairs to the Métro.

"My name's . . ."

"Please," she interrupted. "I don't have to know."

"You shouldn't be sad," he replied. "But holidays can make people sad."

This time she didn't say a thing. She remembered the pills in her purse.

"I'm not a Christian, though," he added.

They went into a hotel that rented rooms by the month, mounting the stairs to his small furnished cubicle at the back of the third floor. He turned on an old marble lamp with a soiled red silk shade. Piles of clothes lay scattered about on the floor, on the desk, on the bed, and when Rosie's eyes widened, he said, "I'm sorry, I'm too messy."

After the cold street, the warm room pleased her. Its radiator burned, hissing hot water. She wondered if he was a student. Books had been stacked high against the wall opposite the door. Some of the titles were in Arabic script, and others in French, although she couldn't make them out.

"May I take your coat?" he offered.

She unbuttoned her coat and he stepped behind her, helping her remove it. "Would you like some coffee?" he asked.

"No, thank you." She noticed several white demitasse cups and a hot plate with two burners on a table beside the sink.

"I don't have any wine," he apologized.

"That's all right."

"I don't drink. But I make good coffee," he said.

"Really, I'm fine."

"Have you ever been to Turkey?" he asked.

"No," she said awkwardly.

On the back of his door he'd nailed a small metal hand, about two inches across, with an eye embossed in its palm. Rosie had seen them before but couldn't remember what they were called. A charm of some kind. Against the Evil Eye?

Abruptly, he touched her arms, moving his hands lightly over her shoulders, and she didn't stop him until he pulled her face up to his and their mouths came together. Her body stiffened.

"I've never seen you in the restaurant before," he said, caressing her fingers as she watched them in his hands. "You don't have to be afraid."

"I'm not," she said.

"You aren't French, are you?"

"No. How did you guess?"

"When you said I spoke good French. They never say that."

She smiled, embarrassed.

He pressed his lips to her hands.

"I am frightened," she said.

"We won't do anything you don't want," he answered, leading her toward the bed. She started to mumble something, but he ignored it.

As they moved away from the light, Rosie began to tremble. She hoped he wouldn't notice, and when they reached the bed she fell onto it, rolling against him. He kept a stack of newspapers almost two feet high beside the bed.

"There," he said. In profile his face seemed less round, and harder.

Rosie found it difficult to breathe; her throat tightened. The pillow smelled of his unfamiliar sweat and stale cologne. She nearly gagged. "I shouldn't have come here," she said passively.

He waited several minutes and then undressed her slowly, avoiding any contact with her skin.

Her breasts were cold, and she wanted to cover them. Without speaking, he began to stroke her arms.

"Please, don't touch me," she said. "I'm not quite myself." People could accept that.

"All right," he said gently.

"I'm sorry."

"It's all right."

"I'm being unfair," she said. The thought that she might tell him about Serge horrified her.

He opened his belt buckle, then his pants, and she waited while he pushed them down to his knees. He was already erect.

"It dances, you see," he said with a self-conscious laugh, and Rosie watched. Unlike Serge, he was circumcised. "I'm dancing for you."

Rosie brushed him away from her thigh with the back of her hand. I don't love anyone, she thought.

"I could still make you some coffee," he offered.

"Do you often bring women back here? From the restaurant?"

He shook his head. "This is the first time."

"Then why me?" He might even be telling the truth, she thought.

"I was watching you all evening."

She looked directly at him; she was no longer afraid. "Because?"

"I liked watching you. Do you mind?"

Exhausted, Rosie closed her eyes. Of course she wouldn't tell him about Serge. The idea amazed her. What an idiot, she thought. Still, she didn't want to know this man or his room. The cheap old drapes covering its window needed mending. By tomorrow, she told herself, I'll have forgotten all of it.

"Will you kiss me?" he asked, without touching her.

She gave him a quick kiss, barely hitting his lips, and was suddenly holding on to him with desperation. The hair on his thighs bristled against her skin.

"I'm not going anywhere," he whispered against her cheek.

A hand of Fatima, she thought. The hand with an eye is called a hand of Fatima. Benyoub had offered to buy her one in Algiers: "It's perfect for you," he'd said. Aunt Pearl had brought one home from Israel, calling it a *chamsa*.

Rosie believed that she would never be able to let go of the man. For a moment there was peace in the world.

They tasted each other's mouth, each other's skin, and after she felt him carefully climb on top of her, push against her, enter her, he said, "My name is Yusuf."

She didn't reply.

"Yusuf Eser."

Touched by his persistence, she said, finally, "And mine's Elza."

20

*T*HE SUBWAY CAR SCREECHED to a halt. It seemed to Rosie that breakdowns on the Métro had become a weekly occurrence. Tonight, on her route home, between the Château Landon and Louis Blanc stations. The wait might be five minutes or half an hour. But she was in no hurry.

She glanced about — at least the crowded car had thinned at Gare de l'Est and she'd found a seat beside an elderly African woman in bright kente-cloth robes and a matching turban. As usual, people avoided eye contact. The regal mahogany woman sat clutching a paper bag between her knees. Slowly, with one hand, she peeled half a dozen pistachio nuts, letting the shells drop into her lap. It was nearly eight o'clock, after a late lesson with a businessman who couldn't get to Continental before six. Most teachers disliked end-of-the-day students, but Rosie didn't object. Not anymore. She reached inside her black string bag, took out a pad of paper and fountain pen, and wrote "May 23, Monday" in the upper right-hand corner. Then she yawned at the nearly blank page. Perhaps she should go to bed early. Deb could wait another day. Yawning again, she stared at the empty page before closing her eyes.

At first Rosie had been stunned. Life continued to be a bad joke, a dirty punch line: "And then she got pregnant."

In the months after Serge's death, her periods had been irregular, so it wasn't until early March that Rosie began to be suspicious. Was her long winter bout of flu actually morning sickness? Exhausted, nauseated, she'd never given a thought to pregnancy.

I want to get out of here, she'd said, at first.

The pills, her insurance, were still in her purse.

But on subways, in shops, in restaurants, she was listening to people, overhearing conversations, watching their faces. A fat woman in a fuschia dress cuffed her small daughter in the neck, saying, "You're being a bitch, Marie, and I don't like it when you're a bitch"; a young man apologized over escargots for another infidelity. Listening, Rosie almost liked the freedom of her own silence. Serge is dead, she thought. *Serge: I'm thinking of you.*

She finally bought new reading glasses, and her hair took on a glossy rich sheen. Pregnancy becomes me, she thought bitterly, without seeing a doctor. It must be the flow of hormones, of course — Rosie knew she wasn't the stoical type. She no longer missed Serge every minute of the day, as if she were about to step into a vast hole. Serge, she hoped, wouldn't mind. Although she carried his notebook in her purse — the last of the notebooks he'd called his examination of the world — she'd been surprised to find it filled mostly with addresses, telephone numbers, book titles and references to newspaper articles, along with an occasional reminder to himself ("Feb. 2. Buy vinegar") or a quoted fragment of conversation ("Renée: 'Capitalists actually lack imagination'"). Serge might even be pleased about the baby, although he'd considered the world overpopulated. How much could one more baby matter? The baby — her baby — belonged to no one else. Deb would suggest naming it after Morris or Elza, but Rosie disliked the notion. This baby would begin life with its own name. Let the past be past. She would always remember it anyway. Her raincoat with the yellow star still sewn on hung in the bedroom wardrobe, beside a trenchcoat of Serge's that she had decided to keep.

At the end of the month she finally saw a doctor, who said she wasn't pregnant after all. A chill ran through Rosie, then relief. The doctor explained that her body's chemistry had gone awry, perhaps from grieving. Was she depressed? Rosie listened passively. "I suppose if I lived in the States I'd be on antidepressants," she said finally. The doctor shrugged and suggested that she watch her diet. "Nutrition is important," he advised. And Rosie felt that she had been given a life sentence: she would end up a useless old woman with a rented stove, a rented refrigerator. But there are many things I can do, she reminded herself: I can conjugate the imperfect subjunctive, I know how to wash dishes, I can make pot-au-feu, I remember my father's birthday, once I memorized the prelude to *Evangeline*. And I'm not pregnant.

She never saw Yusef Eser again, nor did she want to. In fact she avoided the Stalingrad station, and gradually forgot their night together, as she'd hoped she would. "I'm going to badger you," he'd promised, and she suspected he'd meant it; like Serge, perhaps, his sympathies went to people who were at a loss in life.

In early April, Benyoub had invited her to dinner, and brought along a bank draft, proudly, as if it were a rare gift. He promised to telephone again soon, but of course he didn't. As the weather softened, she smelled the mellow scent of the canal, the garbage in the street, and the occasional, unexpected burst of lilacs beside an old building. She didn't want to be tempted by flowers: spring, leave me alone. Sometimes she would stand outside her apartment, looking up at the window. That's where I live, she'd think, but why do I live there? She half expected that one day Thierry would appear to say that he and Renée were getting a divorce, but that hadn't happened yet either.

Serge would ask her what she wanted to do, he would make her decide. "Right now I live to eat," she imagined telling him. "You know that." But I won't gain any weight, she promised herself. There was no place in the world where a woman could be desirably, fashionably fat, with men lined up bearing gifts of Fig Newtons. Not that it mattered. It was too soon to think about falling in love, but love always started there, in a thought. And maybe it doesn't go much further, Rosie mused. She wanted to be done with wanting. With choices and details. Perhaps it didn't matter what kind of meal you ate, what color sweater you wore, if you could name the flowers in a garden, or the constellations, or even had loved one person more than another. You could get lost in wanting, owning, having. So what if she lived in an apartment the size of a postage stamp, she had lived there with Serge. And she couldn't think of another place where she'd felt at home. The days were longer now, and even the air seemed new. Everywhere people gladly sat outside in cafés, sunning themselves. Couldn't that be enough?

Maybe this fall she would take some kind of course — it might not be too late to register. Tomorrow she'd phone the Sorbonne. (She forgot previous courses, all gestures at holding back grim thoughts: French cooking, introductory Spanish, operating a computer.) Somewhere there had to be the right course, Deb had written. She also suggested that Rosie cook dishes that Serge hadn't liked. "Look after yourself," she said. Yet Serge liked everything I made, Rosie thought. We liked the same things. For the first time in weeks she wept, as she packed up his family photographs to send to Odile. Jean Berthelot had persuaded her to return them quickly — he knew it would pacify Mme Deneau and leave Rosie free from pursuit. He visited once a week now, obviously checking up on her, and he tried to amuse her, even imitating Odile's poker face. At the funeral, he said, Mme Deneau had told her daughter that Serge's corpse, laid out in the coffin, didn't resemble Serge, and Odile had replied, "What do you mean? He looks like Serge. Only now he's Serge dead." In spite of herself Rosie had laughed.

Suddenly the subway car lurched forward and its lights flashed off and on again. Rosie opened her eyes. The African woman was gathering empty shells from her lap and wrapping them in a Kleenex. Aware that someone might be watching her, she turned to Rosie and, without smiling, or saying a word, held out the open bag of nuts. "No thank you," Rosie muttered awkwardly, swaying as the Métro car pitched around a corner of the dark tunnel. She had a quick decision to make. She wouldn't get off at the Riquet station tonight, she'd wait for Crimée. It was too late to cook supper and the charcuterie on the corner would still be open. She'd buy some leeks vinaigrette, some smoked ham. Maybe a stuffed tomato.

She would remain in Paris, her home, as much as any place could be. She'd bought a small tin hand of Fatima and hung it over the kitchen sink. Each night, as the days lengthened, as she sat waiting, the familiar apartment seemed to embrace her with all its props of love. She no longer wondered if she should return to Pittsburgh. You can't predict the future, she told herself. A bad joke can turn a somersault; everything seemed possible. But first she would have to learn patience.